THE FIRST TWENTY

What Reviewers Say About
Jennifer Lavoie's Work

"*Andy Squared* is a phenomenal debut…a fascinating coming of age novel that explores coming to terms with sexual orientation, sibling rivalry, and discovering what true friendship is all about, told in very effective prose."—Steven dos Santos, author of *The Culling*

"In her second young-adult novel, *Meeting Chance*, Jennifer Lavoie again applies her hopeful outlook to the halls of high school, this time tackling—and debunking—the superficial judgments on which adolescent self-esteem often turns. Lavoie's assumption that teenagers are strong, smart, and tenacious in the face of life's challenges is refreshing…it serves up a wholesome role model for younger kids to consider as they try to figure out how they fit into the world."
—*Foreword Review of Books*

"*Meeting Chance* is such a sweet story, so full of love. Aaron matures before our eyes as he takes on more responsibility and makes adult decisions about whom he wants in his life. One of the greatest things about this book for me was that although it is a YA LGBT novel, the fact that the main character is gay is a non-issue, for the most part. It's about a boy, who happens to be gay, who bonds with a dog. Ferociously recommended."—*The Novel Approach*

"*Tristant and Elijah* by Jennifer Lavoie was a great read. It was sweet and most definitely a unique high school 'gay' story, because while it did deal with coming out, it didn't go through the usual tropes…it was seriously awesome to read a book about gay high school students where that was essentially a nonissue."—*His Gay Atlas*

"[*Tristant and Elijah*] is an interesting combination of a character-driven romantic story and a plot-driven historical mystery in which the reader learns as much about Tristant's uncle as they do about the two main characters. A conversational writing style and character-driven story makes this novel an easy public and school library recommend for fans of romance literature, especially boys who may want a romantic story without a female main character."—*GLBT Reviews, ALA's Gay Lesbian Bisexual Transgender Round Table*

Visit us at www.boldstrokesbooks.com

By the Author

Andy Squared

Meeting Chance

Tristant and Elijah

The First Twenty

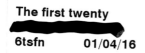
THE FIRST TWENTY

by

Jennifer Lavoie

2015

THE FIRST TWENTY

ISBN 13: 978-1-62639-414-8

This Trade Paperback Original Is Published By
Bold Strokes Books, Inc.
P.O. Box 249
Valley Falls, NY 12185

First Edition: May 2015

CREDITS

EDITORS: LYNDA SANDOVAL AND RUTH STERNGLANTZ
PRODUCTION DESIGN: SUSAN RAMUNDO
COVER DESIGN BY GABRIELLE PENDERGRAST

Acknowledgments

This book would not exist without the help and talents of everyone at Bold Strokes Books. My deepest gratitude to Len Barot for giving Peyton and Nixie a home, Sandy and Cindy for everything they do, Ruth for the help with finishing touches, and Gabrielle for The. Most. Beautiful. Cover. Ever! I hope the girls' story does it justice.

To Lynda Sandoval, who is the best editor in the world, for challenging me and pushing me and making this book the best it can be. It wouldn't be what it is without you! Thank you for your tireless help and support!

To Aleida Gonzalez, thank you for reading the first draft of Peyton's story and giving me feedback and kicking my butt when I needed it.

And as always, to my family and friends who put up with me when I'm writing. I don't know how you do it. Tiffany and Cassandra, thank you for helping me with the title of this book and for giving me Static.

Dedication

For my family, who have stood by me no matter what

CHAPTER ONE

Heat from the afternoon sun burned the back of Peyton's neck as she stood at the foot of her father's grave. Four men carefully lowered his wrapped body into the narrow pit dug into the scorched earth. Most of the security detail stood around her, their arms crossed respectfully behind their backs. Others patrolled the perimeter of the graveyard, scouting for Scavengers.

Scavengers had taken him down.

Peyton would find those responsible for her father's death and she would make them pay. Clenching her fists to keep them from trembling, she pulled herself straighter.

Enrique's shrouded body hit the ground and the crew pulled the ropes out. Peyton reached down, grabbed a clump of dirt, and scattered it over his body without thought. The others followed suit and murmured words she couldn't hear. Remnants of the old days, perhaps. She said nothing as she watched.

When everyone had paid their respects, the four men once again took over and picked up their shovels to bury him properly. Peyton turned to address the security detail that stood behind her, deferring to her for instructions—just as they had once done with her father.

She surveyed those in front of her before nodding tersely. "We need to get back to the Mill and make plans. Let Ryan, Willow, and Jasper stay. They'll provide enough coverage."

The men and women nodded their assent and turned toward home. Ryan muttered something quietly, but Peyton ignored it. Let him moan all he wanted. She would make sure things ran smoothly until someone else took over.

In the distance, the derelict smokestack rose above the distant hillside. A remnant of a time long past, it no longer retained its original function. Now it served as a lookout and communications tower. If she squinted against the harsh afternoon sun, she could just make out the narrow walkway circling the stack and the person left on watch.

Peyton lagged behind. She didn't want to hear any more condolences or make the small talk they all thought she needed. What the hell did they know about what she needed when she wasn't even sure herself? To her dismay, someone joined her. Turning to push whoever it was ahead and away from her, Peyton looked up into kind brown eyes. Graham. He had been her dad's closest friend and sometime lover, and the one who had found his body when the foragers had returned to the Mill without him.

"You held up well today," he said.

She nodded and stared at the backs of those in front of her, unable to speak past the sudden lump in her throat. Graham had lost just as much as her, and still he was kind.

"But it's not over yet," he continued, interrupting her thoughts. "We still need to choose a new head of security. This was the easy part. Now the others will squabble like children."

"My vote's for you," Peyton said after a moment, surprised by the strength in her own voice. She carefully picked over the cracked ground, avoiding the larger fragments of asphalt that remained.

Graham chuckled. "I'm too old."

"My father was your age."

"Maybe so, but he was much younger when he was given the task. No. Not me. I won't accept it."

"If you won't take it, who will?"

Graham's eyes twinkled with amusement. "I think, dear girl, you know the answer to that question." He moved ahead of her swiftly, belying his claim to old age. Enrique had hardly been in his fifties, and Graham was just a year or two older.

It was hard to tell these days, though, just how old everyone was or wasn't. So many had died over the years, and not just from the Mill settlement. Their bodies just couldn't adjust to a life of hard labor after centuries of a sedentary lifestyle. Before, everything they'd needed had been a quick trip to the store or the click of a button away.

Peyton's own parents hadn't survived longer than a few years. Just long enough to hold out hope it would get better, have her, and then die.

So, yes, the first years of the Collapse had aged so many, and those who grew up in the aftermath looked older than they would have Before. Everything was different; it was all Before and After now, and nothing else seemed to matter. At least that's what those who lived Before had told her, and what she'd seen from pictures that had managed to escape destruction. She could hardly believe some of the images she'd seen were of people her age. They looked like children.

As Peyton walked, she looked at the land around the Mill, which had been turned into fertile farmland despite the extreme change in temperature and the former cityscape. Buildings still loomed around her, some well on their way to collapsing, but others, like the Mill, had been built to stand the test of time. Over the years, the settlers had turned the surrounding paved roads, abandoned lots, and empty yards into a large farm that met their needs.

Peyton watched as some of the farmers pulled up weeds or shifted the old tobacco netting hanging above the heat-sensitive plants. They nodded to her as she passed.

If Dad had been a farmer, what would my life be like now? Would he still be alive? Would I be a farmer, too? Or would I have done something else?

Paying attention solely to her thoughts, she tripped over a piece of pavement that hadn't been removed from the road and kicked at it. The pain that spread through her toes and up her calf felt good. It brought her back to her senses and reminded her to keep focused. She took a deep breath, wiped the sweat from her forehead, and picked up the pace to make it back to the cooler interior of the building she called home.

"Calm down, people! We need to make this decision tonight. If we go too long without a new head of security, we're going to have bigger problems with the Scavengers," Julian said before taking a seat. Voices competed to be heard over each other and Peyton tried to discern who said what.

"We already have problems with them."

"Just stick with the schedule and we'll be fine. We can have a few days without. Give us time to think it through."

"No, we need to take a vote. Now. I know who's the best for this job."

"Is that so, Ryan? And you probably think that's you."

"Damn right, it's me!"

"Now wait just a minute!"

Peyton gave up and sat silently in the corner next to Graham, who continued to follow the proceedings with amusement. His eyes shifted back and forth between the men arguing, his lips quirking up at the corners when they pushed closer together and shouted directly in one another's faces. He leaned over to Peyton and whispered, "They're like strutting peacocks."

Peyton hid a laugh behind a hand. It was true. The birds were all show, just like the men—boys—in front of her. Willow sat to the side, hunched over and staring off into the distance with her chin resting on the backs of her hands. Jasper sat slouched, with his head back against the wall. His eyes fluttered closed despite the shouting around him. When Willow noticed, she nudged him with her elbow. He jerked awake and stared around in bewilderment. Peyton had to hide another laugh.

It was the first time she'd laughed in two days, and damn if it didn't feel good, even if the relief was temporary.

The voices continued to grow louder until a loud bang reverberated around the room. Silence settled over everyone uneasily as they turned to look at the source. Old Joe had picked up a cast-iron pot and dropped it on the floor. And now that he had everyone's attention, he pushed himself to his feet with his cane and leaned heavily on it.

"That is quite enough."

His voice, quiet but strong, seemed to settle everyone's nerves and they sat in the seats around the perimeter of the room. Peyton watched with interest as the old man, the oldest in the Mill at eighty, moved to the center of the room. Willow made as if to stand and assist him, but he waved her off.

"Bickering is not what we need right now," he said, addressing Ryan and another man. "We are not savages. It's become clear to me that neither of you can handle the position if you'll fight for it like that. You've only yourselves in mind." Both men hung their heads. "Losing Enrique is hard. He was the best we've had for security since the Mill was settled. But we'll pull through this. We always have. What we need is to be democratic about this and vote."

Peyton stared at Old Joe. He'd used that term so many times, and she'd had to ask the two teachers in the Mill what it had meant the first time he used it. They'd handed her an old history book from before the Collapse, and she'd read about what the United States of America used to be. Sometimes this idea of democracy worked, and other times, she found, it made no sense. Not when there were too many competing minds and no one wanted to give in to the other side, even if giving in made everything better for others.

That's what Old Joe had said started the Collapse. That and shifting weather patterns that caused worldwide crop failures, and diseases that spread too rapidly for scientists to keep up.

When he said her name, she blinked and looked around the room. Everyone regarded her with open curiosity. She licked her lips and Graham nudged her shoulder.

"Say something."

"I wasn't paying attention," she admitted through clenched teeth. She glanced at Willow who beamed at her with an easy smile.

"Old Joe just cast his vote for you."

Peyton whipped her head around, balking at the words. "What?"

"Stand up," Graham hissed.

She did as she was told and stood. Old Joe's eyes crinkled as he smiled. "The only person who knows all of Enrique's techniques and plans is Peyton. He trained her well, and she is the most sensible choice. She has proven time and again that she is capable, and I think she'll follow in her father's footsteps just fine. Besides," he chuckled, "I think she's the only one who can make sense of the maps he's drawn out."

"That's ridiculous!" Ryan erupted from his seat and stalked to the middle of the room. "She's too young! She hasn't gone on nearly as many missions out of the city as some of us."

"Are you suggesting that you'd be a better choice?" Jasper asked from his seat, finally alert. "Because you're *so* much older and wiser?"

Ryan scowled.

"Are there any other candidates we should consider?" Old Joe asked, turning in a circle to take everyone else in.

Peyton turned with him, eyeing the others. She didn't want the task to fall to her, but she didn't want Ryan to take it, either. He thought only of himself, and not of the others. She'd experienced his cruelty when they were children, and it had not matured out of him as he aged. All of her dad's hard work would be destroyed if Ryan became the head.

Did she want that to happen?

In the room, fourteen men and women sat still. The others were on the night watch already. There were two others in the room she would rather take the lead, but Graham had already told her he wouldn't. When Old Joe looked at him, he shook his head and looked at the ground.

That left Julian. Peyton turned to him, but he shrugged before saying, "No. I'm happy remaining in security, but I won't run it, not when it'll take me away from the Mill. With Avery being pregnant, I'd rather not."

"You're our best chance, Julian," Peyton argued.

He laughed. "No, I'm not. Enrique was our best chance. With him gone, it's Graham or you."

"You'd take an old man over me?" Ryan shouted, gesturing toward Graham. His face turned red in the dim light of the room and Peyton saw a flash of hatred flicker over his eyes. Graham stood tall, his usual calm gone.

Julian was arguing with Ryan now, in defense of Graham. Old Joe slammed his cane onto the ground three times, calling their attention back to him.

"Shall we vote, then?" he asked. A murmur of agreement rippled through those gathered and Peyton stayed at his side. Ryan took up position to his right, his chin tipped up as his eyes flashed around the room.

"Those in favor of Peyton for new head of security, raise your hand."

Peyton glanced around at the room and watched as Graham, Julian, Willow, Jasper, and five others raised their hands as if they were back in the schoolrooms. Nine for her. She raised her own hand, casting the tenth vote. There were only eighteen members of the security crew. Old Joe went with the formalities anyway.

"Those in favor of Ryan, raise your hand."

The remaining five members in the room raised their hands, including Ryan. He shot her a glare.

"I'll speak with the three currently on duty tonight to see what their votes are and let you know of the official decision in the morning," Old Joe said as he shuffled out of the room, seemingly eager to leave.

Those who had voted for her stood to offer their congratulations and encouragement. She didn't hear it as she stared at Ryan, whose eyes never left hers.

"Don't worry about Ryan," Jasper said in her ear. "We've got your back."

"I'd still be careful," Willow warned from her other side. "He's got his friends. He won't make this easy for you."

"Nothing ever is easy," Peyton said softly, finally breaking eye contact with Ryan as his friends led him from the room.

CHAPTER TWO

I thought I told you not to come back until you got what we needed!" Faulkner yelled from his makeshift shack.

Nixie sat on the ground outside, trying to listen quietly. Bark pressed sharply into her back at an awkward angle, making her position uncomfortable, but she was afraid to move. If she didn't move, didn't make a sound, they would just leave her alone.

She was tired. The trip had exhausted her. The dowsing had exhausted her, and it hadn't been worth anything anyway. All the water they'd found had been impure and needed filtration equipment— equipment they didn't have, equipment they were supposed to steal from the Settlement they'd found.

But they couldn't get it, and when they'd run across a group of them...

Nixie shuddered despite the heat. She'd never seen so much blood before. The stench had been so strong that, for the first time in her life, she hadn't been able to sense any water. And the man who had been killed...she frowned at the memory, still too fresh, and wondered if it would ever fade. Who had he been? He shouldn't have tried to stop them, really. It was his fault he was dead. The so-called Settlers should share with everyone else. Nixie scowled. There were so few people left compared to Before, at least according to Faulkner, so why shouldn't they all work together and pool resources? What was a little filtration equipment when they could probably make more anyway?

The blue tarp that created the doorway to Faulkner's shack pushed aside and Ranger emerged. He shot a brief, narrow-eyed glance her way before striding off in the direction of his own shack.

"Nixie!" Faulkner roared. The tarp shoved aside again and his grizzled beard preceded him. "Get in here."

She scrambled to obey as quickly as possible. Of all people to cross, Faulkner was not the one. His hand may have been firm and tyrannical, but at least he kept the people in line. She'd heard horror stories from Travelers about times when they'd run across a group with no clear leader. They were better off this way.

"Yes?" she asked timidly as she entered, not needing to duck like the others to get into the shelter.

"What the hell happened out there?" He settled into an armchair. Stuffing protruded from a tear in the cushion, and stains covered much of the once-yellow fabric. The tinkling of glass followed as he settled back and stretched his feet out. One of the dozens of glass bottles surrounding him tipped over and rolled toward her. She brushed it to the side as she kneeled on the dirt floor.

"We found water, but when I got closer, I realized it wasn't pure. No amount of boiling would have made it safe to drink. It had some sort of…chemical in it." She waved her hands vaguely, gesturing toward the ground.

"Fine, but what about the equipment? How hard can it be to steal from a bunch of foraging Settlers? They're like a pack of yearlings out here."

"They had a guard with them. He spotted us first."

"And you killed him. So where's the goddamned equipment?"

Nixie cringed. She was sure Ranger had just explained it all, so why did he ask her now, too? Was he trying to corroborate their stories? Make sure they weren't lying? Why would they?

"There were more of them than there were of us, and the guard blocked our attempts to retrieve—"

"I thought you said you killed him."

"Before he died. He didn't die right away."

"One guard against the five of you. Really?"

"I don't know. I'm just supposed to find the water." She spread her hands wide and hunched in on herself, trying to become as small as possible. "I'm not trained to fight." It was the one thing her mother had argued against, claiming it would dull her senses when it came to the dowsing. What had that lack of skill cost them?

Faulkner sighed and hung his head, muttering under his breath. Nixie could barely make out the words, but she heard a faint *useless witch* mixed in there.

It wasn't the first time she'd been called that, and it wouldn't be the last.

"We need that equipment to survive. I don't need to tell you how hard it is to find clean water around here."

"I understand that, but if we moved farther north, I think—"

"We're not moving. We have just as much right to this land as they do."

"I know," Nixie quickly stated, trying to defuse the situation, "and I know you decide what's best for us, you always have, but other groups have said food and water up north are more plentiful, and—"

"We're going to raid their settlement and take what they won't share." Faulkner ignored her. He stood up and paced the few feet between his walls.

Are you insane? Nixie wanted to shout. They hadn't even managed to get what they needed with the five in their party against a bunch of foragers and one guard. How would they manage to get inside their settlement and find the small device they needed to live? *Has the madness spread to him?* she wondered, eyeing him nervously as he continued to pace. His lips moved soundlessly.

"Faulkner, I'd never question your decision, but is it wise to go after the filtration unit while it's still inside their walls? I mean, after what happened, killing one of the guards, they're probably more protected than they were before."

"They won't expect it. It's bold. They're complacent when they're in those walls. They're just as bad as people from Before." He sneered and Nixie shifted back on her knees. "Yes, this will work. Go," he said after a moment. "Tell Ranger I need to speak to him again. We have to plan. This time we won't fail."

Nixie scurried from the shack as quickly as she could. Outside, the camp had settled into its nightly routine, with mothers boiling water to sanitize it and preparing meager meals for their children.

Ranger wasn't at his shack. She asked the others if they had seen him pass through, but most just shrugged and went about their business. Weary, disappointed eyes were turned back toward their food.

Word had already spread around the camp that she hadn't found water.

Finally one of the children spoke up. "I think he went huntin' with Harper," he said from his mother's feet.

"Thanks," Nixie said quietly, offering him a smile. It was all she could give him at the moment.

Nixie sat down at the edge of the camp, just beyond the ring of trees, and settled in to wait. She wouldn't go after them now; no way would she end up on the pointed end of their weapons like that guard had. With Ranger in a foul mood after talking to Faulkner, she wasn't sure he'd stop even if he knew who it was.

Trying to make herself as comfortable as possible, Nixie rested her chin in her hands. Her thoughts drifted to the others in the camp. They needed her to find clean water. These people who had become her family needed her, and she'd let them down. How much longer could they survive without a new source of water? Supplies were already so low. Nixie could feel it in her pores, in the way they tightened. She felt dry, as though her skin would crack from the gentlest of touches.

Tilting her head back, she closed her eyes and breathed in deeply. If she concentrated hard enough, she could just make out the faint scent of the water from the cooking fires. In the air above her, though, was a different perfume. This one sang of gentle showers and plenty. Crisp and cool. Green. Alive.

The rainstorm teased her. Small tendrils reached out in all directions and tickled her senses until her body vibrated from the pleasure of it. If they could have, her bones would have cried for it in welcome. But it was just that. A tease. The scent had been lingering in the air for the last two months with not a hint of the rain it promised. Faulkner had even gone so far as to send out scouts in the cardinal directions to track it after she had told him what she sensed. They'd all returned exhausted and without news.

Nixie wondered if her desire to find water was overriding her abilities and making her mad.

"Hey. Wake up." A rough hand shook her shoulder sharply and Nixie's eyes snapped open, all of her senses alert. She stared up at Ranger as he looked down at her, a mixture of amusement and momentary concern in his eyes. "What, you sleeping under the stars now or something?"

"What?" Nixie asked, then looked around. She'd fallen into a trance waiting for Ranger to get back from his hunt, and she'd let her own concern get the better of her. "Did you get anything?" She saw the rabbit attached to his belt immediately after voicing her question and felt dim-witted.

"You shouldn't be out here alone," he said simply, letting go of her shoulder and making his way toward camp.

Nixie stood, scraping her palm on the tree bark in her haste to follow. "I was waiting for you. Faulkner. He wants to talk to you." She'd nearly forgotten what she had been doing under the tree in the first place.

Ranger grunted. "'Bout what?"

"He wants to raid the Settlement."

"That so."

She hesitated before she voiced her concern. "I think…maybe the madness has gotten to him."

Ranger spun on her, grabbing her by both shoulders and stooping to her height. She gaped up at him, frightened.

"Who else have you said that to?"

"N-no one."

"Good. Keep it that way." He let go, and she rubbed her left shoulder, wincing.

"But, Ranger—"

"But nothing. Don't say a word. Don't worry about it. If you're right and he has been touched, I'll deal with it."

Nixie stared after him as he walked away, letting him put more distance between them. If Faulkner had been touched, if the disease that seemed to creep up on the aged among the Travelers affected him, then the group could be in trouble. She'd heard tales whispered from people who never settled with one group, tales about entire groups of people destroyed by the foolish actions of a leader touched with madness. Sometimes she wondered just how much truth was in the tales of these people who preferred to be alone. Were they just stories told for a free meal and dry shelter for a night? But there had to be some truth in it. How else would so many of them mention the same thing?

Besides, she'd heard Faulkner's crazy idea earlier. And if Faulkner were going down that road, they shouldn't travel with him. If they did, they were all vulnerable.

CHAPTER THREE

The apartment Enrique and Peyton had called home was too large without him there. Peyton turned around and took in the towering ceilings and covered walls. A few old maps of the city hung, the hunting trails etched out in red. Dad had altered the maps over the years as buildings fell and territory was claimed by other settlements. Would the task of keeping track of decay and potential hazards fall to her now that he was gone? Wouldn't it be better to have one of the hunters keep track of the trails to monitor game movement? If she did accept the vote and take the position, the first things she'd change were the responsibilities of the group members.

She glanced around at all of his other possessions. He'd been a collector, always finding something while out on security detail to add to his shadowboxes. He'd found the boxes in old buildings or made them from scraps of wood. Some of the other residents had called him a Scavenger because of his hobby, and she had grown up hating that, thinking they were insulting him. But Dad laughed it off. She could still hear him saying, *Not a Scavenger. Just a collector of lost art.* His lost art just happened to be little trinkets found on the trails.

He'd always talked when they were at home, as if he couldn't stand the silence. When he had first taken her in, he told her stories about the little odds and ends he'd picked up, making up tales of who they'd belonged to or what they were for. When she was little, she had believed everything he'd said, and the stories became a comfort to her. But as she grew, she knew not all of the tales were true. It had been nice, though, to hear about the good people whose items he reclaimed to keep them safe.

What would she do without him? For the first time since his death two days before, his absence loomed like a shadow as the sun faded and a darkness settled over the apartment. Solar-powered lights that had charged during the day slowly flickered to life, and she knew she couldn't stay there. The silence weighed on her heavily.

Bolting from the lonely rooms and choking down the sorrow she had managed to suppress the last few hours, she headed for the large tower at the front of the building. At six stories, the structure made it possible to see far into the distance, though most of the residents didn't bother with it, claiming no air moved through the large, paneless windows.

The sun had disappeared from the sky and the moon hung over the tower, watching everything below it. Though the heat from the day waned, it wouldn't dip low enough to cool anything off. They needed a rainstorm, and they needed it desperately.

Peyton tried to distract herself with these thoughts as she paced around the tower room. A stray breeze blew through the window and whipped her hair around her face. She pushed it back and her hand caught in a knot. Tears formed in her throat and she tried to swallow them. How stupid to get frustrated by a knot in her hair! A sob tore through her and she settled against the ledge, allowing the tears to finally fall after holding them at bay for the last two days. Dad was gone, and he was never coming back. He'd left her alone, just like her first parents. Alone to fend for herself in a world gone horrifically wrong. She wasn't sure how long she'd sat there, tears running down her face, when a creak in the floorboards alerted her to another presence. She sat up, alarmed, and swiped at her eyes.

What luck if Ryan catches me like this. She couldn't let any weakness show; he'd find some way to manipulate it.

"At least it's a cooler night than it has been." Graham's kind voice instantly set her back at ease and she turned to him. He said nothing about her tear-streaked face. Just paced around the room, looking out the windows and checking on the landscape, then smiled and stood at her side.

How like him.

Peyton enjoyed his silent strength as the moon rose a few degrees higher in the sky.

"There used to be a saying. Before. That tears are not a sign of weakness. Just a sign that you've been strong for too long. My grandmother told me that. The only time I saw her cry was when my mother died. She was a strong woman, and my mother being taken was too much."

"You never talked about your mother before."

Graham chuckled softly. "No, I guess I haven't. She died in the first wave of disease. We were too poor to afford health care and she wasn't vaccinated. I was only ten years old."

"I'm sorry."

"Don't be. She didn't suffer. She didn't have to see the world fall apart."

"But you were young," she said, turning to look at him. The shadows hid his face, and it was hard to read him.

But he's always been hard to read.

"You were young when you lost your parents, too. So much younger. You know, sometimes I think everyone who died, they're the lucky ones. We might be alive, but we're stuck in this hell. But then other days I think maybe we were chosen because we're strong enough to carry the world and make it a better place."

"Chosen? By who? Are you talking about God?"

"No," Graham said with a shake of his head. "Not God. I stopped believing in God a long time ago. Just fate, I suppose. Or destiny. Whatever you want to call it."

"I don't believe in that."

Amusement colored Graham's voice as he agreed with her. "No, you never have. Always the cynical child of the bunch. Jasper was the dreamer. Still is."

Silence settled over them again, and Peyton watched as the stars, so bright and vivid in the sky, seemed to pulse. Like they were giant fireflies far in the distance.

"What do you miss the most about the world before the Collapse?"

Graham tilted his head as he thought about it. "The noise. The food."

Peyton looked at him, startled, and he laughed.

"Oh, I know you've heard that the food was bad, and it was. Bad for you, but so good anyway. The restaurants we see as shells used to be filled with people, every day. When I was seven, my mother took me to a restaurant with a buffet. She told me I could have whatever I wanted. Peyton, you wouldn't believe the amount of food there. I piled my plate so high and carried it back to my seat. I barely ate any of it, though. It was too much. My eyes were bigger than my stomach." He laughed again at the memory and shook his head.

"I get the food, but the noise?"

"Yeah. I grew up in the city and fell asleep every night listening to horns beeping and people shouting. Sometimes it's too quiet now. But at least you can see the stars."

"What foods do you miss?"

"Chocolate." He sighed. "And pineapple. The real tropical kind, not what we've started to grow here. It's not the same. What I wouldn't give to have those again. My mouth is watering just thinking about them."

"I wish I could try real chocolate. Just once."

"Maybe someday you will. Someday we'll get the world connected again. You'll see."

"You're so optimistic."

"Can't afford not to be when everything looks so grim." He settled a hand on her shoulder and changed the topic abruptly. "I miss him, too."

"I know."

"If you ever need anything, you come to me."

"I will," she said. "Thank you."

Graham turned to leave. She heard the creaking of the boards as he walked to the ladder leading down to the fifth floor.

"Graham?" she called out. He turned and looked at her, an eyebrow raised. "You loved Dad. Why didn't you get married?"

For the first time in her life, she saw tears in Graham's eyes, and it was unsettling. Graham was calm. He was the quiet to Dad's constant chatter. The logic to Dad's fantasy.

"There was no need to rush. We always thought we had all the time in the world," he said quietly, his words hanging between them. "I guess we were fools. When you get the chance, Peyton, you have to take life and live it, before it gets away. Don't make the mistakes we did. Don't live your life to have regrets."

CHAPTER FOUR

I can't believe we're doing this tonight," Nixie whispered. Her lips pressed to Ranger's ear, trying to be as quiet as possible in case guards were out in the woods around them.

They lay prone on the ground in dense foliage. Ranger's darker complexion made it easier for him to hide in the shadows, but Nixie's pale skin and hair had to be covered with an extra layer of clothing. The hat covering her head made her sweat in the heat, and she shifted slightly to swipe at a drop rolling down her cheek.

"Faulkner wants a status report. He thinks they won't be expecting anything so soon after that guard's death, and...I'm inclined to think he's right," he muttered reluctantly. "For once."

The Settlers' compound sat before them at the base of the hill. The grounds were quiet and dark, with just a few solar lights indicating the path into the building, like a beacon of welcome.

Nixie knew better. If she were to waltz up to their door and ask for help, she'd be turned away. For as much as the Settlers claimed to help others, the claim was false. She had experienced firsthand their cruelty when her mother was sick and needed shelter. The settlement had turned them away, and her mother had died because of it.

The large square tower before them rose above the building proper. Through the open windows a pair of silhouettes paced. Were they guards? She checked the shadows but didn't see any weapons. Maybe not. Nixie nudged Ranger and gestured toward the tower with her head. He glanced in that direction and held up two fingers and then spread his hand wide, palm up.

Had she seen just the two of them?

She indicated that was all she had seen, and together they watched as the taller silhouette retreated.

The moon rose slowly above them, shifting shadows and revealing details. Nixie's eyes started to droop at the utter stillness. Reconnaissance had never been her strong point, at least not compared to her dowsing, and she wondered why Faulkner had insisted she accompany Ranger. The Settlers' water situation was just as desperate as theirs. She'd allowed her sense to expand and felt the trickle of the cool stream. But it was just that. A trickle.

It didn't take someone with dowsing abilities to figure that out, though. The lack of rain was proof enough. No water supply could keep up indefinitely without being replenished.

Ranger nudged her and jerked his head to the side. He'd gotten enough information and they were finally leaving. Once they made it back to camp and they gave their report to Faulkner, she would be able to sleep and recharge her energy before he sent her out for another dowsing.

Inching backward along the ground, the two of them untangled themselves from the brush. Once behind a tree and out of direct line with the building, Nixie stood.

"They had just the one guard, it seems."

"They're definitely complacent," Ranger replied. "The death might have thrown them off balance, but they don't expect anything else to happen. I almost feel bad for them." He chuckled.

"You feel bad for them?"

"I said almost."

Nixie followed behind Ranger, letting him navigate their way. She watched his feet as they picked over bared roots and large rocks. Doing her best to avoid them, she only tripped once.

"Careful," Ranger warned. "Don't need you to break anything."

"A little fall isn't going to break a bone," she said indignantly once they had crested the hill.

They remained silent the rest of the trip back to camp. By the time they arrived, the sky had begun to lighten. The camp was still, though, with the gentle sounds of sleep coming from each tent and shack. Fires had died down to a few coals. One dog picked up its head as they passed and huffed, blowing out his large jowls.

Faulkner was the only one awake. He sat outside on a raggedy strip of carpet staring into a crackling fire. Had he been awake the whole time they'd been gone? He didn't give them a chance to greet him. As soon as they were close enough, he motioned for them to sit and barked out a terse, "Report."

"They didn't have any extra guards out. Just saw one sitting in a tower." Ranger left out the other one they had seen initially while he drew out a map of the complex in the dirt and pointed to where they had seen the silhouettes.

"Lazy bastards. But that's good for us. We can move on this tomorrow."

"Tomorrow?" Nixie asked, her eyes widening.

"We need the equipment. They won't be expecting us so soon. The guard's body is barely cold in the ground, so now's the time to do it."

Nixie glanced at Ranger. He kept his eyes firmly on Faulkner, not betraying a single thought through his emotions.

"The two of you will go, and take four others with you."

"Just six?" Nixie gasped. "To raid the entire compound? We don't even know where they keep anything!"

"When you get there, create a distraction. I don't care what. Nixie, I want you in that building. Use your talents to find the equipment."

"But it doesn't work like that! I can only find—"

"Water will be left on that equipment. Do whatever you do to find it."

Nixie turned to Ranger for help. "But that's not how it works!" she insisted. "I can't just focus on a small remnant of water. It's…it's just not how it's done."

"I don't need to tell you how important this equipment is to us." Faulkner's eyes narrowed as he focused on her. "Figure it out. You leave at sundown."

CHAPTER FIVE

Old Joe delivered the news to Peyton the next morning. She had officially been chosen as the next head of security.

"Your father would be proud of you," he said with a gentle smile. "Never doubt your ability to lead."

The first thing she did was meet with the heads of the foraging and hunting groups to discuss the maps her father had kept, but there had been no need. Her father's maps were actually copies of their maps that he kept updated.

"Why?" she asked the two men.

"Need to know where you guys'll be escorting us," one responded with a shrug.

I hadn't thought of that. Dad would have figured that one out. Scowling, she pushed her way out of the building and ran into Jasper. He leaned against the railing of the bridge, surveying the farmers working in the closest lot. His blond hair hung in his eyes, desperate for a trim.

"How goes it, great leader?" His face split into a grin.

"Don't call me that."

"Someone's in a mood."

A mood? Probably. So much had been handed to her overnight—things she didn't want, wasn't ready for. She could have said no, but that would have left Ryan in charge, and that just wasn't an option. "I didn't sleep well," she admitted. She hadn't slept soundly since Enrique died and probably wouldn't for a while, either. Everywhere she turned, memories of him haunted her.

"Well you better snap out of it or Ryan's going to be on you like flies on honey. And not in a good way, if you know what I mean."

She rolled her eyes. "Knock it off. Where's Willow?"

"Probably out flirting with that guy that moved here from crosstown last month. He is pretty cute, isn't he?"

"I wouldn't know."

"Oh, that's right. Because you can't take the time to look. Looking doesn't hurt, you know." Jasper followed after her like a puppy as she strode across the bridge. Her longer legs left him jogging to keep up, though he kept his hands shoved in the pockets of his baggy jeans. Peyton gave him a sidelong glance and realized he looked thinner. He'd lost weight again. She'd have to talk to the kitchen to get him extra protein.

"I adjusted the schedule for the next three days. I'll be covering most of Enrique's work detail, but Graham is covering the rest until I get the mess sorted out."

"You'll have to talk to Lynda. Find out when she's sending her gnomes out foraging again so you can assign a detail to them."

Peyton paused and looked at him. "Don't let Lynda know you're calling her foragers gnomes. She'll have your balls."

"Well, she can't have them. I'm saving them for someone special."

Peyton felt the laughter bubble up from her chest and burst out. It was hard not to laugh around Jasper. He had a gift for saying just the right thing at the right time to get himself out of trouble. Always had. Graham called it a silver tongue once, and after that, Jasper had walked around for a week straight trying to convince people he really *did* have a silver tongue. He had even gone so far as to invite the boys to see it for themselves.

They found Willow helping some of the farmers irrigate the crops. The water level of the river had gotten dangerously low in the last few weeks, and Peyton chewed at her lip. She'd heard some of the farmers telling Old Joe they didn't know what they'd do if the water ran out. She glanced to the bridge they'd just crossed and could barely see the water. What used to be freely flowing now trickled sluggishly past, barely covering the tops of the rocks.

If the water really did run out, they'd have to rely on whatever the foragers found, and what was kept in storage. But could they find enough to feed nearly 150 people? And what would they do without something to drink? Graham told her the human body couldn't last much more than three days without liquid.

They needed rain, and they needed it to last a long time.

"How's it going?" she asked when Willow stopped her work and ambled over to them.

"It's going," she said, wiping the sweat off her brow. "The water level is too low for the pumps to work."

"I guess we're going to have to save our dirty water and use it to water plants, huh?" Jasper said, making a face.

"Well, if we have to, they'll let you know. But it might be a good idea."

"I figured we'd find you with that new guy."

"Christopher? Why?"

"Because you're in love," Jasper said, batting his eyes. Willow gave him a playful shove and he nearly lost his balance but grabbed her arm and regained it. "For that I'll tell him you're abusive. Maybe he'll cozy up to me instead."

"Sorry, Jazz, but I don't think he swings that way."

He sighed heavily and shook his head. "I'm starting to think no one does. I'll have to go crosstown or something."

"What about that guy who came through last year? He wasn't so bad. He seemed to think pretty highly of you, anyway." Willow laughed.

Jasper scowled and spat into the dirt. "Those people are nearly as bad as the Scavengers." He paused then squinted up at the sky as if considering. "Besides. Then I'd have to leave the settlement and travel. I'm not cut out for that stuff. I want to stay in one place. Plus," he added as Peyton and Willow started to walk away from him, "you would miss me too much!"

"What I wouldn't do to shut him up," Willow muttered.

"Next time a foraging group is going crosstown, I'll put him on the detail," Peyton whispered.

"Thank you."

Willow returned to aid the farmers in getting the crops water while Jasper joined her for a scout around the perimeter of the Mill. By the time they returned, the sun was fading from the sky. An idea that had worked its way into Peyton's mind was out of her mouth before she could stop it. "I want to go after the Scavengers. Take them out before they can get any more of us."

Jasper stopped walking, forcing her to stop as well. His eyes narrowed. "What do you mean?"

"I want to get rid of them."

"You mean, like, push them out of the area?" When Peyton didn't answer, Jasper jerked his head back. "Are you fucking crazy? We can't do that! We'd be just as bad as them."

"They're not going to stop," Peyton said.

"Maybe not, but we make it harder for them. Look, I know you're upset about your dad—"

"Upset?" Peyton barked out a laugh.

"Okay, you're hurt. You want to kill. I get that. But you can't. You couldn't do it alone, and someone else could get killed. We don't even know how many there are."

"Five."

"Five when Enrique was killed. That doesn't mean that's all there are. We don't know what we'll be walking into." Jasper grabbed her arm. "I'm worried about you."

Peyton jerked her arm out of his grasp. "He deserved better."

"I know. But there's nothing we can do."

"That's not good enough!"

Jasper winced. "Maybe not, but think. Would your dad want us to risk our lives to get back at them?"

As much as she didn't want to admit it, Jasper was right. Enrique would never have encouraged revenge. A breeze rustled the leaves around them, and Peyton thought she heard the familiar voice she'd never hear again whispering *Let it go, Peyton.* But how could she?

"Where's the justice?" Peyton whispered before she could bury the words.

❖

The shrill alarm pierced the night air and jerked Peyton from sleep. She launched out of bed and shoved her feet into her shoes without a thought as she made for the hallway. Outside, chaos ensued. People stumbled out of their homes, confused by the noise.

"What's happening?"

"Is it a fire?"

"Mommy, I'm scared!"

"Where's Julian?"

Voices rose as the hall filled and panic set in.

"Out of my way!" Peyton yelled, pushing her way to the stairs. She needed to get down to the security office, figure out what was going on.

She didn't go far before someone called for her by the stairwell.

"What's happening?" she asked Julian.

"Scavengers! They broke through the perimeter and made it into one of the storerooms!"

Peyton cursed loudly and followed Julian's tall frame through the path he made. At the mention of Scavengers, murmurs rose through the crowd and they parted to let Peyton through.

"How did they get in?" she demanded as they took the stairs down two at a time. "What did they take?"

He shrugged. "We just know they got into the storerooms. Ryan and Bill caught them as they were leaving."

"Where are they now?"

"I don't know. Ryan went after them. Sent Bill to get me."

Peyton followed him as quickly as she could, thankful the other residents pressed against the sides of the hallways as they sprinted down the corridors. They rounded a corner and caught up with Bill, who pointed them in the right direction. "Are they armed?"

"Couldn't tell."

Peyton followed just behind Julian. She had no weapon with her, and there wasn't time to go back and get one. Together they exited the building, hopped the low fence, and followed the broken branches. Someone had fled through there in a hurry and hadn't bothered to cover their trail. Peyton heard shouts to her left and she changed direction, with Julian almost glued to her side. The sounds grew closer. Peyton pumped her legs harder, overtaking Julian as she rounded the bend and came upon the river just as she heard one last shout and a splash.

Ryan stood on the bank holding a shotgun. If the situation hadn't been so desperate, Peyton would have chewed him out for having a restricted weapon, but at the moment, she had bigger fish to fry— namely the Scavenger glaring up at her from the riverbed.

CHAPTER SIX

Everything had gone so well until Nixie tripped on an exposed pipe as they were leaving the compound. The noise had attracted the attention of the guards, and then everything went to hell. Ranger had grabbed her arm and pulled her to her feet, but she was slower than the rest. It wasn't long before she'd fallen behind and had the Settler at her heels. She changed direction, hoping to throw her pursuer off Ranger's trail.

Faulkner had wanted a distraction, hadn't he?

She didn't know she was at the river until it was too late. Her momentum carried her forward and she'd tumbled headfirst into the shallow water. Her knee wrenched and she bit back the scream of pain. When her vision cleared, the Settler stood over her and she was looking down a long barrel. The others were long gone. She hoped they'd made it out with the equipment.

Other Settlers appeared at the first one's side and she froze. Was this it? Would she die now? At least with the filtration device, the rest would be able to survive without her.

"Get her out of the water and bring her back to the Mill," a young woman, probably close to her own age, said. She stood at the edge, barefoot and wearing clothing that suggested she'd been pulled from her sleep.

"What about the others?" the one with the weapon asked.

"We'll get them later."

Another man stepped forward and climbed into the river. He wrapped a large hand around her biceps and pulled her to her feet roughly. Nixie bit her lip to keep from screaming as her knee locked.

Two of them managed to get her out of the river, and she stumbled as they pushed her to walk back down the path she had taken. Nixie took a step and her knee buckled. A short yelp escaped her lips before she clamped down to hold it back. Ranger's words echoed in her mind: Never show fear or pain.

"Dammit, Julian, carry her or we'll be here all night," the young woman commanded. She had to be their leader—why else would they follow her order without hesitation? Nixie was lifted off her feet and tossed unceremoniously over a broad shoulder as if she weighed nothing. Compared to the man who had lifted her, she weighed no more than a toddler.

Back in the Mill, she was brought to a damp, windowless room. The solar-powered lighting blinded her when it was flicked on and she squinted against it, trying to gain her bearings. Much like the storage room, the ceiling towered over her, but this room was smaller and mostly empty. When her eyes finally adjusted to the dark, she made out the shadows of boards and bricks tossed haphazardly in the corner.

"What did you come for?" the young woman asked, looming over her.

Nixie glared up at her. She pressed her lips tightly together and refused to answer. There was no way she would tell them anything about Ranger and the others. The longer she held out, the more time they had to get away.

"She's not going to talk," the one with the weapon said. He laced his fingers together and cracked them. "Might as well beat it out of her."

"Get out."

"What?"

"I said, get out, Ryan. You're dismissed."

"Wait just a minute—"

When the leader spun, her blond hair whipped around her shoulder. Strands had come lose from the messy ponytail she had it tied up in. For the first time since her capture, Nixie had time to study the girl.

Loose linen pants clung to her tall but curvy frame. An extra-large T-shirt hung from her shoulders, torn in a few places and advertising, with a faded logo, some once-popular musician who would have died decades ago. The shirt shifted and revealed one smooth, tanned shoulder. She stood with an air of command, like Ranger did when he was giving orders, and when she put her hands on her hips and drew her shoulders back, she seemed to grow another few inches.

The guy with the weapon, Ryan, turned to leave the room without another word and had just disappeared when she added, "And leave the shotgun in the office. We'll talk about that later."

She turned back to face Nixie. Her face didn't betray emotion as she approached. Nixie wanted to press her back against the wall, but she held her ground.

"What did you come for? What did they take with them?"

Nixie bit down on her tongue.

"You might as well answer because you're not going anywhere."

"You can't keep me here."

"And why's that? Is there an appointment you need to keep?" The curve of her lips suggested humor, and if it weren't for their differences and the dire situation, Nixie imagined she might enjoy bantering with her.

The leader began to pace the floor. "So what is it? Food? You couldn't have made off with much of it. Tell you what, let's play a game. I'll mention a few things you could have taken, and you'll tell me if I'm getting hot or cold."

"Why should I tell you anything?"

"So it couldn't have been food." She ignored Nixie's question and addressed the man she'd called Julian earlier. "What's in that storeroom?"

"Mostly equipment," he said. "Spare tools, extra parts, scrap metal."

"Scrap metal would be too heavy to carry. So what tools did you take? What parts?"

Nixie leaned back on her hands, ignoring the throbbing in her knee as she shifted. The concrete under her palms scratched at her skin. The strong odors of mold and mildew stung her nose.

"I can do this all day."

"Peyton, maybe we should let her cool off for a bit. She might talk more after a few hours down here with the rats."

Nixie laughed. "Rats. Terrifying."

Peyton turned and got down on her level. "No, the rats wouldn't bother her. They're scavengers, just like her." Peyton stood, looking down at her over her nose. "But at least the rats don't have other options."

❖

"How long are you going to keep her down there?" Jasper asked. He leaned back in his seat and clasped his hands behind his head. He had his feet up on the low table, ankles crossed. To Peyton, he seemed completely at ease except for the small bounce in his foot.

"As long as it takes her to talk."

"That's all well and good," Graham said, "but what if she doesn't talk?"

"She'll starve if she doesn't."

He rolled his shoulders in a lazy shrug. "We are talking about a Scavenger here. Hunger isn't anything new to them. She may be so used to it, she doesn't talk. And what will that get you? A dead Scavenger."

"The only good Scavenger is a dead one," Ryan muttered, as he entered the room.

Peyton rounded on him. "How the hell did you get a shotgun last night? Those are for emergency situations only."

"This was an emergency."

"So you're telling me you had time to go back to the office, unlock my father's cabinet, and take out a shotgun before going after the intruders?"

"Enrique isn't here anymore, and neither are Enrique's rules. There's no reason to keep everything locked down tight. Clearly we need to protect ourselves." Ryan flung out a hand, encompassing the room. "If you're not going to do the job right, you should pass it on to someone who will."

Pressure built in Peyton's temples. She wanted to rub them and ease the headache, but she couldn't show that weakness to Ryan. Instead she pulled her shoulders back and steeled herself. "If you're not going to answer my questions, get out of my office," she demanded, stressing that it was, in fact, her office now. When she stood up straight, she was nearly nose-to-nose with Ryan, so his attempts at intimidation were useless.

He opened his mouth but snapped it shut like a fish and then dropped into his seat.

Peyton turned back to Graham. "So if I can't starve her out, what should I do?"

"Show her some respect and kindness."

Ryan barked out a laugh and Peyton found herself smirking with him. "You're joking."

Graham's eyebrow twitched up. "I'm not. The easiest way to get her to talk is to treat her like a human being. If you treat her like shit, she's going to clam up and not give you anything."

Jasper rolled his head to look at her and shrugged. "It couldn't hurt. What's the worst that could happen?"

"We use our time and resources to plump her up and get nothing?"

"Well, that's just a risk you'll have to take. Make your decision, Peyton. You're our leader now."

Peyton stood outside the medical ward, waiting for Dr. Easton to finish speaking with her young patient. The child held up his finger for inspection and Dr. Easton clucked over it.

"My, that is a nice splinter."

"Are you gonna hurt me?"

"Taking it out?" she asked and then shook her head. A sweep of gray hair fell from its clip and obscured her vision. "Well, that all depends."

"On what?"

"On you. Do you want it to hurt?"

"No!" The boy laughed. "That's weird."

"It is weird. So, if you don't want it to hurt, it won't hurt." She smiled and glanced over at Peyton. She winked before turning back to the boy. "After I take it out, can I keep it for my collection? Or do you want it back?" She picked up a pair of slender tweezers and pinched his finger with her other hand, bringing it close to her face.

"You collect them?"

"Yes. Would you like to see my collection?"

"Gross, no—hey!"

"All done," Dr. Easton said with a chuckle. She set the tweezers down on her silver tray, swabbed his finger with disinfectant, and then stood. The boy stared at her. "Off you go. Be careful when you're climbing next time."

"Thank you!"

Peyton moved out of the way as he scampered past her. "I remember the first time you told me about your splinter collection."

"Works every time. What can I help you with? You seem well enough."

"Observant as always, Doc. It's not actually for me. It's for our guest."

"The Scavenger?"

"Yeah. Last night when we brought her in, Julian had to carry her. She fell into the river and I think she broke something."

Dr. Easton pursed her lips. "And you waited this long to tell me?"

"I didn't know what we were going to do with her. Can you take a look at her? Maybe fix her up a bit?"

"Of course. Let me get my kit. If she broke a bone we'll have to bring her back here so I can set it."

"Can't you do it there?"

"I will not treat a person in a damp storeroom." She gathered her materials and placed them in a black canvas bag.

"But she's a Scavenger."

Dr. Easton turned to Peyton, and despite her shorter stature, her glare made Peyton feel like a child again. Her usually warm brown eyes were cold and distant. "You're Enrique's child, but you have a long way to go before you are a leader like him, Peyton. He would never leave a person caged like an animal, Scavenger or otherwise. Now, let's go."

CHAPTER SEVEN

Nixie did not expect the older woman who opened the door. She hadn't expected anyone to come so soon after her lockup. She examined the woman warily as she entered, toting a bag with her.

"Don't worry," the woman said. "It's just me, no guards. I've been sent to check you out. I hear you're injured."

Nixie raised an eyebrow. "Hospitality from a Settler?"

The doctor set the bag down. "I'm a doctor first. Settler, Scavenger. Makes no difference to me. An injured person is an injured person. Now, let's take a look. Peyton said you're a little battered."

"I fell into the river," Nixie admitted.

"How do you feel?"

Ranger's words not to show fear or pain reverberated through her mind, but she pushed his voice away. This woman was a doctor, and like it or not, she needed help, so she took a leap of faith. "My knee hurts. I can't put any weight on it."

"Let's take a look then." She smiled. "I'm Dr. Easton, by the way."

"Nixie."

"What a lovely name." Dr. Easton stretched out both of Nixie's legs, checking first the uninjured one. She ran her fingers up the muscles, then switched to the other leg. She gently probed her calf. "Tell me when I reach a spot that hurts."

Nimble fingers danced up her leg, pressing gently at first and then with more pressure. There was a slight pain in her calf, but Nixie didn't say anything. That's not what really bothered her. When Dr. Easton reached just below her knee, a short hiss escaped her lips.

"There?"

"Yes."

"Okay. It's definitely swollen. You did a number on it. But it's not broken," she said as she slowly pressed her fingers into the area.

Nixie bit her lip to keep from crying out. "How long will it take to heal?"

"That depends on you. If you rest and keep weight off of it? At most, a couple of weeks."

"A couple of weeks?" Nixie cried. A couple of weeks meant she'd be trapped with the Settlers, relying on their kindness—or lack thereof. She had to get out of there.

"Yes, a couple of weeks. If I can convince Peyton to move you to the medical ward, it'll be easier to take care of you and get you back on your feet sooner."

"How soon?"

"If I can get some meds in you and keep it iced, then a few days."

Nixie's pulse slowed down and she breathed a sigh of relief. A few days was manageable. She could do it. Of course, she'd still have to rely on them for food, but if she could just hang in there she'd be out the moment an opportunity presented itself. *If I let them think it'll take longer to heal, then they won't be watching me as closely and I can get out.* "Do you think she…Peyton…will let you help me?" Nixie looked down at the ground. "She doesn't seem to like me very much."

"Can you blame her?" Dr. Easton chuckled. "You're a Scavenger and your people stole something from us. Besides, it's more than just that."

"What more could it be?"

Dr. Easton rocked back on her heels and looked into the distance. "Peyton had something precious taken from her recently. By Scavengers. And she's angry."

"Taken?" As the word left her mouth, realization dawned on her. *The guard we killed.* Nixie grew dizzy as the blood rushed from her head.

When Dr. Easton looked back at her, her eyes narrowed in focus. "You look ill. Did you hit your head when you fell? I should check for concussion."

"No," Nixie said, holding her hands out in reassurance. "No, I didn't hit my head. I'm just hungry," she lied.

"Then we need to get you something to eat. Let me put a brace around your knee. It will stabilize it for now until we can get you comfortable. Then I'll get you moved to medical."

Nixie watched as she worked. She packed up her materials efficiently and then shouldered the bag. "Peyton is outside. Should I get her to help?"

"Why are you being so nice?"

"I'm a doctor. It's my job to help people."

"You said it yourself. I'm a Scavenger."

Dr. Easton stared down at her before holding out a hand. "My dear, I was training to be a doctor when the world went to shit. I took an oath to help people, no matter what, and that's what I'll always do. Regardless of who or what you are."

Nixie stared at the hand offered. If she had any hope of getting out of here, she'd have to trust someone. The most logical choice was the doctor. She seemed genuine and so far had done nothing to suggest she would ever be otherwise.

Dr. Easton arched one pale eyebrow and Nixie realized she had kept her waiting for far too long. She held out her own hand and didn't flinch when the doctor took it. The older woman smiled at her, and Nixie returned it.

Maybe if I keep her on my side, I can get information out of her.

"What do you mean you're moving her?" Peyton demanded as soon as Dr. Easton finished speaking. It didn't matter that the Scavenger, Nixie, was standing there propped up by the doctor. She frowned as she flicked a glance toward her and then away.

"She needs to rest in comfort or she won't heal. I'm not leaving her in a damp basement. Doctor's orders overrule yours, Peyton. Your father knew that."

Again her father. Peyton missed him and wanted to make him proud with her leadership, but it seemed like everything she did, someone brought him up and compared her actions to his. She forced her shoulders to relax. "Fine. Let me get Julian to help move her."

"We'd be fine if you helped."

Nixie shifted her weight and looked at the ground.

Peyton rolled her eyes and took a step toward her.

"All right, Nixie, just keep your foot up for now and let us do the work. Feel free to step down on your good leg," Dr. Easton said.

Peyton slid an arm around her thin waist and stooped. "Put your arm around my shoulder."

Nixie raised her arm and placed it on her shoulder. Peyton hesitated before reaching up and holding onto her arm so she wouldn't slide away. She was so slight, her arm thin and bony, and her narrow waist was more boyish than anything with next to no curves. Peyton shook away those thoughts. She didn't care if the Scavenger fell. It would serve her right.

Together they made it to the medical wing without much incident. En route, they'd run into Static, who appeared curious and interested in something other than his radios for once. He disappeared without question the moment Peyton shot him a glare, though.

"Set her down on the bed carefully," Dr. Easton instructed once comfortably inside her domain. She set the bag down and unpacked her supplies, then moved around like a whirlwind, collecting other things.

Peyton turned to find Nixie staring at her. "So…is it broken?"

"No," Nixie said, crossing her arms. "Thank God for that."

"Thank God? God has nothing to do with it."

"It's just an expression."

"Ah. So you don't practice the old religions?"

"No. Of course not."

"Neither do I," Peyton admitted. "Not many of us do."

"Same with us. Scavengers, I mean." She hesitated before adding, "There are a few that still do, but I never understood it."

Dr. Easton interrupted and handed Nixie two large pills and a glass of water. "Take these. They'll take away the pain and help with the swelling." Nixie stared at the pills.

"Don't worry, they go down easier than they look," Peyton found herself admitting. When the Scavenger gave her a faint smile, she stood up straighter. *Pretty smile.*

"The water is delicious," she said, eyes closed.

Peyton might not be one for religion and praying, but the look on Nixie's face when she drank the water and swallowed the last drop reminded her of the few old ones left who prayed fervently every Sunday. "It's just filtered water," Peyton said. "Nothing special."

The trance that held Nixie seemed to break as her eyes snapped open. The short peace they'd struck between them broke. "Just filtered water? Do you have any idea how many people don't even have steady access to water, let alone clean water?" Her pale blue eyes narrowed until Peyton could no longer see the color. "You Settlers are all the same. You have no idea how bad it is out there. People are still suffering and you hoard everything you have without sharing. If you'd just let us have—"

"I think Nixie needs to rest," Dr. Easton interrupted.

Nixie stopped her ranting and turned away, effectively shutting Peyton out.

Peyton felt the sting of disappointment. She thought they'd made a tenuous connection, like her father would've done. She took the doctor's advice and left the medical ward to give Nixie space and privacy. Outside the door she ran into Static, who skulked in the hallway.

"What are you doing out of your cave?" she asked as he tried to peer around her shoulder beyond the doorway. Peyton blocked his view as the heavy door clicked shut.

"Wanted to get a look at the Scavenger. Maybe talk to her."

"Why would you want to talk to her?"

Static shrugged. "Find out what she's seen out there. They usually travel a bit, right? Maybe she's seen some of the pieces I need."

Peyton rolled her eyes. "You need to get out there and get the pieces for yourself. No one is going to find what you need. We don't know what any of it looks like!"

Static pulled a piece of wrinkled paper from his torn jeans. He looked at Peyton quickly before glancing back down at the sheet. "If you'll just take a look at the list."

Peyton sighed and took the paper. She read over the items quickly to humor him. "Static, I still can't read this."

"But if you could pass it on to the girl."

She shook her head and gave it back to him. "Look, just leave her alone. Doc says she needs to rest. I don't want to hear from anyone that you've been buzzing around." The pathetic look Static gave her reminded her of a puppy left out in the rain. It was hard to say no and turn away from something like that, but she just raised an eyebrow and walked away. She didn't expect him to, but Static followed after her, running a hand through his spiked black-and-gray hair.

"But the radios will work if I can just get these parts. We can get them going again and connect with other settlements farther out. Maybe start to rebuild instead of just existing. And it'll be faster to get messages to Ox Farm and Ellington!"

Peyton didn't break her stride. "You said the radios have to be two-way."

"Well, yes. Of course. The other side has to have one."

"But what if they don't?"

"Then we get them one! But someone out there has to have a working radio. I'm sure of it. I'm just an amateur, but there are experts!"

"I hate to burst your bubble, but billions of people died, Static. There might not be any experts left. We don't even have Maverick anymore."

His lips flattened at the mention of Maverick, but he merely said, "There are *always* experts left. Somewhere. You just need to have faith."

Peyton stopped and watched as Static shuffled off to his domain of rusted parts. She'd never given his obsession much thought; no one did. But maybe he had a point. Maybe they needed to devote some time to finding these old parts before they completely disintegrated. He had a knack for turning what looked like a heap of scrap into something that worked. If there was some truth to what he said about connections, maybe she should send a guard out with him to finally help him find what he needed. At the very least it would keep him occupied for a few weeks while she dealt with their guest.

CHAPTER EIGHT

G uilt racked Nixie every time she downed a glass of water. It tasted so fresh and the doctor brought her plenty of it. Sure, they might have been hit hard by the drought, too, but clearly they still had reserves if they were letting her drink as much as she wanted. At times she felt like a glutton. And when she was given the opportunity to soak in a hot bath and scrub the filth from her body? She couldn't even remember the last time she'd truly bathed like that. All that water, just to get clean.

Days had passed since she'd been captured and no word from Ranger or the others. Had they gotten what they needed and Faulkner decided to give her up? It was true they'd be able to filter the water they found and make it safer for drinking, but how would they find the water without her? Worried, she brought her thumbnail to her teeth, gnawing until she had bitten down to the quick. She winced at the raw skin but couldn't find it in her power to stop.

A light knock on the door mercifully drew her attention away from it. The door slowly opened and Peyton poked her head inside.

"How are you?" she asked, her eyes taking in Nixie as she reclined on a bed with a pristine white sheet over her.

The Settler's voice was like water in a cool, bubbling brook. As much as Nixie wanted to hate her—and *did* hate her for what she represented—that mellifluous voice had begun to soothe her nerves and put her at ease.

She hated that power.

"Better. Dr. Easton said I should be able to walk by the end of next week," Nixie stated. Despite her kneejerk notion to bluff the guards about her injury, she'd come to realize it was pointless to hide the truth from her. The older woman would have told Peyton everything.

From her time with the good woman, she'd learned that Peyton was the new head of security, and everything important to the Mill went through her and the other group leaders. Nixie had been intrigued by how they all seemed to cooperate with one another to get things done. It was so unlike her people. Faulkner held total control over everything. He dictated when and where people hunted, when and where they foraged, and when Nixie should search for water. She had been given free rein over the where, but that was only because of her ability, and she had no say in who would make the travels with her.

"That's good," Peyton said, shutting the door behind her. She took a step farther into the room and glanced around, hesitating before taking one of the open seats.

"If you're looking for the doctor, she was called away."

"I know."

Oh. Now was the time for her interrogation, then. She pulled her lips back in what she hoped was a sneer. "Someone waiting outside, then? Ryan perhaps, with his shotgun?"

"No," Peyton responded, one eyebrow arched. "Why would he be?"

That took the wind out of Nixie's sails. She frowned. "Then why are you here?"

"Checking up on you."

"Why?"

Peyton leaned forward, resting her arms across her knees, and spread her hands. "You're in our care, now. As the one who…took you in, I need to make sure you're okay."

"That's not the impression you gave that first night."

One shoulder shrugged and Nixie detected the trace of a blush on her face. "I guess that was…the heat of the moment." She dragged a hand over her face, looking tired. "I was dragged out of sleep and I hadn't exactly gotten good rest for the few days prior."

Nixie could sympathize with that, though she knew the cause of her sleeplessness was different from Peyton's. Nixie had too often gone to bed without food, sometimes without even water, and she'd lain awake for hours, her stomach rumbling loudly every time she breathed, or her lips cracked from dehydration. She'd begun to wait out the early morning hours when the dew clung to leaves and she could suck the moisture from the plants.

"So you took it out on me."

"What would you have done in my place? You were an intruder. It's my job to protect these people."

"Before that, it was your father's position." Peyton looked stunned as she said the words, and Nixie appreciated being able to bring that look to her face. "Dr. Easton told me." A pause. "I'm sorry about your father."

"Scavengers killed him." She paused, letting those words land like a hammer blow. "Do you know who did it?"

Nixie looked down at the sheet covering her, picking off a piece of nonexistent debris. "No. Sorry. There are other groups out there. Perhaps it was one of them." Why did lying to Peyton feel so wrong? She was a Settler. They didn't give a shit about her people. They'd just as soon pick them off as kill a deer for food. So why was she having such a hard time meeting her eyes again?

"Your parents must be worried about you. I'm sorry for that," Peyton said after a few moments of tense silence.

"My parents are dead." Nixie looked over to find Peyton's eyes wide in surprise. "I never knew my father, and my mother died when I was young."

"Mine, too. I mean, my birth parents," she admitted when Nixie tilted her head, confused. "My parents came to the Mill after I was born. They were sick with the disease that killed so many people. I should have died, too, but I didn't. I guess, by then, the strain was weakening, or we were getting stronger. I don't know. They died and Enrique took me in. He raised me." Peyton laughed and it was a hard, bitter sound. "I don't know why I'm telling you this."

To know she had something so personal in common with the Settler unnerved Nixie. She clenched the sheet in her hands and twisted it. "Thank you for telling me," she said when the silence grew unbearable. "I guess we're not that different after all."

The sound that came from Peyton's mouth was half laugh, half snort. "Maybe not, but that doesn't change what you did."

"No, but we all have our reasons, don't we?"

"So what was yours?"

And here it comes. The interrogation. Nixie straightened her spine and tore her eyes from the sheets to focus on Peyton. She wouldn't show fear. She was strong, despite what Faulkner might think of her.

"The health and safety of my people are my reasons. Everything I've done since I came of age has been to help them survive."

"So what are you? You can't be a hunter. You're too small."

"Size doesn't always matter. Skill does."

"Sorry, but I just can't see you killing something, even to help your people." She said the words with the bite of scorn in her voice.

Nixie put as much force in her voice as she said, "And why is that?"

"Because you're too…nice."

Well, that was a surprise. Nixie stared at Peyton as she processed what she said. "I'm too nice?"

"Yeah." Peyton waved a hand through the air, a frown tugging at her lips. "I can't explain it, really. I mean I don't know you, but you just seem like the kind of person who couldn't do that. Scavengers don't farm, so you must be a forager."

In a way, she was right, so she nodded. Peyton's eyes lit up as she smiled in triumph, and Nixie's heart skipped a beat.

Weird.

But the imposing guard looked completely different when she wasn't scowling or brooding, and it wasn't a bad look at all.

"If you're a forager, why were you on the raid?"

Peyton might have skill, but she wouldn't get Nixie to talk so easily. "We don't have the luxury you Settlers have. There aren't as many of us as there are of you. We all hold multiple roles in the camps. Life is much harder outside these walls."

"Do you think it's easy inside them?"

Nixie gestured to the white linens and the clothing Peyton wore. The denim might have been worn in some places, but the patches had been made by a skilled person. Her button-down shirt had matching buttons, all still attached—something Nixie never saw on her people. She'd never cared what she looked like; her appearance was secondary to her ability. But next to someone as beautiful as Peyton, she felt inferior. "What do you think?" The feeling of calm she'd had while talking to Peyton dissipated only to be replaced by the sting of something she couldn't identify. She lay back down on the bed, closing her eyes. Peyton said something, but she couldn't make out her words, and after several moments the door opened and clicked shut.

She was alone once again.

CHAPTER NINE

Nixie will be ready to move in a day or two. She's healed a lot faster than I would have thought," Dr. Easton said as she sat across the desk from Peyton in one of the folding chairs, four days after Peyton's visit to Nixie. The chair wasn't comfortable, Peyton knew from experience, but then visitors to the office weren't encouraged to stay long and chat. There was always too much work to do.

"That's good to know. Thank you for telling me." Peyton looked back down at the schedule she'd drawn up for the next few weeks of work details. When the doctor didn't leave, she looked up again.

"What are you going to do with her?"

"What do you mean?"

Dr. Easton sighed. "You can't hold her here forever, Peyton. What are your plans?"

"We need to find out what was taken and if the others will be back."

"Considering no one has figured it out yet, do you really think it's necessary? Can't you just let it go?"

Peyton straightened in her chair, frowning. "If I let them get away with this, they'll think they can come over here and steal from us all the time."

"Yes, but if you go after them, I'm going to have a bloody mess to clean up. You don't know what life was like Before. I do. These conflicts never end well."

"They can't feel free to take whatever they like from us. You must see that."

The doctor rubbed a hand across her forehead and sighed. She looked exhausted and Peyton wondered how her student's training was coming. The woman needed a break.

"I know. I see it. That's the problem—it's a catch. We're damned if we do, damned if we don't. So again I ask, what are your plans?"

"We need to get her to trust us. If we can win her over, then she'll feel obligated to help us."

"You think she'll feel obligated to help the people who've been holding her prisoner?" Dr. Easton snorted. "I doubt that."

"You've nursed her back to health, haven't you? She must trust you."

"To a degree, yes. But her loyalties will always lie with her people. Think about it from her perspective."

Peyton tried to put herself in Nixie's place. It would be hard, if not impossible for her to trust the Scavengers, but she'd also appreciate the freedom to move. If they were to show her some trust, she might be able to trust them. "As soon as she can move, I'll give her freedom to roam the Mill."

Peyton didn't need to look at the doctor to know she raised her eyebrow in astonishment. "Freedom to roam the Mill."

"With a shadow, of course."

"Doesn't sound like freedom to me."

"She won't know she has a shadow."

"Who do you suggest might be that skilled?" Dr. Easton asked.

Peyton smiled. "Graham, of course."

Graham stared at Peyton blankly for a moment after she finished telling him her plan. She held her breath as she waited for his reply, worried he would reject her idea outright.

"I guess that's as good an idea as any," he said after she felt as if she'd turn blue from waiting. "If I'm to be honest, it sounds like something Enrique would suggest."

She released the breath she'd been holding and it came out louder than she'd expected. It was the first time since she'd taken over that someone suggested an idea of hers bore any similarities to her father's, and she felt the swell of emotion just before it pricked her eyes. "If anyone can get her to trust us, it's you."

"Thanks for the vote of confidence, my girl. It's good to know I still have some use in me yet."

Peyton narrowed her eyes. "Of course. You're an important part of the Mill. Has someone said something to you? Ryan?"

"Don't be so quick, Peyton. There are just days I feel my age, is all." He waved his hand dismissively. "So what exactly are my orders?"

"Accompany her around, talk to her. Make her feel comfortable—"

"But watch her for any signs of flight. Got it. Where will she be staying?"

That was something Peyton had been trying to figure out for days, but as yet, she still had no solution to that particular problem. They didn't have a free apartment open for one person, and she couldn't trust her to be alone even if they had.

Graham came up with the perfect solution. "She can stay with me. I have plenty of room and I'll be able to keep an eye on her for longer periods of time."

"She won't have to know you're security. Graham, that's brilliant!" Peyton threw her arms around him, relieved. He returned the hug. It felt nice to have human contact. She'd never been one for it as a child, but now that Dad was gone, she regretted not going to him more often.

"So," Graham said as he pulled away from her, "when do I start my new duties?"

"As soon as we get her out of there. A day or two if she doesn't do anything stupid to wrench her knee."

"Then I'll go clean the extra bedroom. It's been a long time since I've had a use for it. You wouldn't believe the mess."

Peyton watched him walk away. She had work to do as well. The rest of security would need to be alerted to the release of their prisoner, and she knew a few people who wouldn't take it well.

CHAPTER TEN

Well, Nixie knew they weren't going to just let her go when her knee had healed, but she hadn't been expecting such a friendly person to be taking her in. She stared at the older man, Graham, who offered her a room—her very own, he assured her—in his home. She'd never had a room of her own, and the idea appealed to her.

Even if it was temporary.

Over the course of the last two days she'd realized she would have to gain their trust and make them believe she wanted to be there, to be a part of their society. Once she had freedom to come and go at will, she would sneak out at night and find Ranger and the others. It had been a week. Had they even tried to come and get her? The thought was uncomfortable and Nixie pushed it to the furthest reaches of her mind. She wouldn't think of it now. Of course Ranger would try to get her back. There was no way Faulkner would just let her go, filtration equipment or not.

When Peyton had visited her earlier that morning, she'd forced herself to be as pleasant as possible, inviting her to sit down and offering to get her a glass of water before the guard spoke to her. "We don't have any spare apartments to give you, but one of the residents has agreed to let you stay with him for the time being."

Nixie didn't allow herself to ask how long she was expected to stay there. Instead she forced a smile and said, "How kind of him."

Hours later Graham came to take her to his home, and she was taken aback. She had expected someone much younger and, well, bigger. Like that guard—Julian was his name—who had carried her that first night. He would have made sure she didn't run. Did they really trust her? As Faulkner would have said, she wouldn't look a gift horse in the mouth. Whatever that really meant.

"You'll have a few days to adjust to life here. I'll show you around, let you get your hands dirty in a few areas, and then you'll have to start helping out. To earn your keep, of course. Everyone works here."

"Of course," Nixie said. "It's the same with my people. Everyone has a job."

"What did you do there?" he asked as he led the way up the stairs.

"Forager," she told him, just as Peyton had suggested during her interrogation.

"Excellent! Me, too," Graham said with a kind smile. His eyes seemed to brighten as he spoke. "If you decide to continue that path, we can go out together. You'll be a great asset to our community."

Nixie had been an important asset to her people, a necessary one, even. But she couldn't tell him that. While she was here, she had to keep her dowsing abilities a secret. Who knew what these people would do if they found out. Graham's apartment was on the fourth floor. From the outside of the Mill, there appeared to be only four levels, but once they stepped through the door, she realized she had been wrong. The ceiling came down much lower than in the other sections she had been in. When she stepped farther into the room, closer to the windows, she realized there was another floor above them.

"That's where the bedrooms are," Graham said, gesturing to the open staircase tucked into the corner of the apartment.

"Wow. It's much bigger than I thought it would be," Nixie admitted. "Are they all this big?"

"Some are a little bigger, some are smaller."

"But it's just you. Why do you get one this large?"

Graham shrugged. "I've lived here for many years. This is where I chose to live, and no one has asked me to leave yet." He chuckled.

"Were you ever with someone?" she asked, looking into what had to be the kitchen. She stopped and stared in awe at the equipment he had.

"No, never was. There's food in the fridge, though I'll have to get more since there are two of us now. But don't worry about that."

Nixie reached out to touch the handle of the fridge. She'd seen them in abandoned buildings and she knew their purpose, but she'd never seen one that worked.

"Go ahead. You can open it. It won't bite," Graham said with a chuckle.

She grasped the handle and pulled it open and couldn't hold back the gasp that escaped her. The inside was a pristine white like the sheets in the medical ward, and food sat on each shelf. A burst of cool air filtered over her and she closed her eyes, enjoying the feel of it. Breathing in, she could smell the fresh fruits and vegetables and her mouth watered.

"How? How does it still work?"

"Many years ago, After Collapse, the original Settlers of the Mill found solar panels from abandoned buildings and set them up. They're on the roof, if you'd like to see them. They harvest energy from the sun and store it. All the working appliances run on the solar energy. It's what enables us to function off-the-grid, as they say, since...well, since there is no grid anymore."

"What do you do for water?" Nixie shut the door and stared at it.

"The sinks still work. Though, you should conserve the water. Don't let it run too long. There are tanks in the basement of the building that store water, and we collect rainwater when it falls. Pumps run on harvested energy carry it up to the apartments. There's also a large tank off to the side of the building that was built during the first twenty years After Collapse. It helps with the water pressure. Let me show you the bathroom."

"All apartments have bathrooms? How is that possible?"

"After Collapse, the public sewer system began to fail as many of the workers died. Some managed to keep it running as long as possible until those left could convert to another system. Every apartment in this building has a composting toilet. I was here when they started to install them. Believe me, it's a wonder that they did. Before, everyone had to use a pit latrine built toward the woods, away from us. That was after the sewer system began to fail. It wasn't pleasant."

"My people use them," she admitted quietly. "I thought everyone did. I thought only Dr. Easton had one because of her patients."

Graham opened a door and showed her the bathroom. There had been something larger in it at one time, likely a sink and cabinet like she had seen in some buildings, but it had been ripped out.

Nixie's mind reeled from everything she was seeing. Why didn't her people have a solar panel? How large were they? If they were to have one, it would solve so many problems, like keeping their food fresh for longer periods of time. They'd be able to store it until it could be used. They could change their lifestyle. None of the children would go to bed crying because they hadn't had enough to eat. What about these toilets? There were days when even though the latrine was far from their camp, the stench reached them and caused her to gag.

Yes, her people enjoyed living outside of solid walls. They felt more at ease not being enclosed. Some had said that the walls felt like a cage, but if they were to have one solid building to store appliances like this, with a solar panel on top, it would fix so many pressing issues.

Why hadn't someone thought of this before?

Why hadn't Faulkner?

Peyton stared out the window and watched Graham and Nixie as they made their way around the complex. She stood just far enough back in the shadows that she wouldn't be seen if either of them looked up, but she knew that Graham had to be aware of her watching. She had to watch, in order to make sure the girl didn't try anything. It had nothing to do with the way Nixie moved, or the shine of her skin after she'd been cleaned up. She looked so fresh and young. Graham must have said something funny because her lips quirked up in a faint smile. At least she thought it was a smile. From this distance, it could well have been a grimace. Was her knee really healed? "Why do you care?" she whispered bitterly to herself.

Jasper approached her position and lounged against the wall. "How's it going with the Scavenger?" he asked, yawning into his hand.

"I haven't been able to talk to Graham yet, but it seems to be going well. He was a perfect choice for this."

"Really he was the only choice. Who else would you have stuck her with? Ryan?" Jasper snorted. "One of them would be dead by now, and my bet is actually on Ryan."

"Why's that?" Peyton asked, moving to another window as the pair below them moved out of sight.

"Well, I've been thinking about how she came to be here."

"You were thinking? Shocking." A tiny smile pulled at her lips.

"Ha-ha. But seriously, don't you think it's odd that one of them fell behind and got left? That she fell into the river? I mean come on. She had to have known it was there."

"She said she misjudged it."

"And you believe her? All I'm saying is, it's strange. Just think about it, okay? I could be wrong, but what if she's here to scope out the place? What if they have other plans and she's just a plant?"

Peyton turned to Jasper. The thought had crossed her mind, but there was something about Nixie that she couldn't shake. Something different. She was tough and headstrong, yes, but she didn't fit that role. Maybe her size was lulling Peyton into a false sense of security, but she really didn't think that was the case. "I'll keep what you've said in mind, thanks."

"Just trying to look out for you, boss." Jasper grinned and gave her a weak salute, then slunk off, presumably to find someone else to bother, like Willow.

As Graham showed Nixie the beehives they kept, Peyton approached. She wanted to talk to the two of them and see how things were going, but she had to maintain her composure. She didn't want Nixie to feel like she was being checked up on for security purposes. Just a friendly chat. At least that's what Peyton hoped for.

"Don't get too close, or the bees will come out and swarm," Peyton warned.

Nixie turned, her eyes narrowing briefly before she flashed a quick smile. Closer to her, Peyton could see how the smile transformed her face and made her look relaxed and even younger than before. "I've been stung before. Don't worry, I'll never get too close again."

"You've been stung?"

Nixie nodded. "I was telling Graham about it. When I was little, I'd heard that honey was sweet, and I wanted to try it. My mother had warned me about bee stings, but I was hungry and wanted something to eat. So I found a hive with some of the other children from my group. We couldn't climb the tree, so we thought we'd knock it down with rocks. The first one hit and the bees came out." She chuckled. "It hurt then, and I was scared, but now that I think about it, we must have looked funny running away, screaming, arms swinging wildly."

Graham laughed with her. "It's a good thing you weren't allergic to the venom."

"Yeah, I was really lucky."

"Did you ever get to taste the honey?" Peyton asked.

She shook her head. "Not then, no. But a few years later a Traveler came through with honey and we traded for some. We each got a little, to use as we pleased. Most people put a dollop at a time in their tea to save it, but I ate my spoonful straight."

"Worth it?"

"So worth it." If the flash of a smile before had transformed her, this one made her radiant. Peyton had to turn her head to look away before she was drawn in. Her pulse sped up and she struggled to slow it down. Her cheeks tingled with the beginning of a blush. *What the hell?* She coughed and turned away, pretending to survey the building. "I spoke to Old Joe about increasing your allotment," she told Graham. "He said to go down and take what you needed."

"Thank you, but I could have done that myself."

"I know. Just helping out."

"Very thoughtful of you," Graham said. "I know you must be incredibly busy with other more pressing matters."

She shrugged and kicked at the ground. "Did you show her the recreation rooms?"

"We were headed there next," he admitted.

"Good. When you're done, I also spoke to Avery. She said she'd be happy to lend Nixie some clothing for the time being since she won't be wearing it anytime soon."

"Why's that?" Nixie asked.

"She's pregnant and she doesn't fit into her old clothing. She's a little taller than you, so they might be a bit big, but they should work."

"Thank you, I appreciate it."

Peyton hesitated. She had no idea how old Nixie even was. For all she knew, she could be fourteen. Based on her size, she looked even younger. "We could try to get you some smaller clothing, from the children," she started but trailed off when Nixie crossed her arms.

"I'm not a child," Nixie said, hotly.

"Easy," Graham said, resting a hand on her arm. "She doesn't mean to offend you. It's just that you look young." He grinned. "Take it as a compliment. It was a compliment, Before Collapse."

"Except now, young means weak," Nixie said, her tone biting. "I'm eighteen."

Well, that's definitely not what I thought. "I thought you were—" Peyton cut herself off and nodded, trying to smooth things over. No need to ruin any progress they might have made with a jab at her looks and age. "Sorry. I didn't mean to upset you."

"Young does not mean weak here. Not to us," Graham explained as if Peyton hadn't even spoken. "We have several young members of the Mill who hold very important jobs. Like Peyton. She's also eighteen."

Nixie jerked her head back to stare at Peyton, who nodded.

"Oh," was all she managed. Her demeanor shifted as she looked down at the ground, her face coloring.

Was she embarrassed, too, for the misunderstanding? *How old did she think I was?* Peyton didn't want to ask.

"Come along, Nixie. I think you'll be pleasantly surprised with what I have to show you next," Graham said, gently touching her elbow and guiding her away. "We'll stop by and speak to Avery after and get you something more comfortable to wear."

Nixie threw her one last look over her shoulder.

Peyton stayed and watched them as they wandered along the path back to the Mill, wishing she could be there to see Nixie's face when the recreation rooms were revealed to her. She wasn't sure why she wanted to see Nixie's reaction. Peyton's imagination supplied her again with the image of Nixie's bright smile, and that only confused her further, especially when it made her chest warm and tight and sent tingles to her palms.

CHAPTER ELEVEN

Graham opened the recreation room door and ushered Nixie inside. Like the main building, the ceiling was tall, with the original beams and exposed brick walls. Equipment sat behind a low partition that barely cleared her head, and tall mirrors hung from all of the walls.

"What's this for?" she asked, walking into the center of the space and staring at everything.

"This is the gym. Everyone comes here to exercise. It helps us maintain our health, even if we aren't going out to work every day. Some use it to relieve stress. It makes us stronger."

Nixie leaned down and saw a row of weighted bars. She picked one up with a soft *oof* and read the side. "Ten pounds."

"Those are weights. There are many things you can do with them."

She nodded and put it back, spinning to take in the rest of the equipment. One looked like a bicycle, but where it would go, she had no idea. Some looked like they would be better for torture than relieving stress.

"There's one more area I think you'll enjoy. Come with me."

Nixie followed him as he walked down the narrow path to the door on the opposite side of the building. She blinked into the bright sun as he opened the door and stepped through, gasping in surprise. Her skin tingled as it sensed the clear water before her.

"There's so much water!" she cried in disbelief.

Around the water people lounged in chairs. Children laughed, tossing a ball back and forth. One approached the water, let out a yell, and jumped in.

"He'll pollute it!" she said in horror, reaching forward to snatch him out of the water. Graham stopped her with a hand on her shoulder.

"No, it's all right. This is a pool. It's meant to be used like this."

"But what about drinking? How can you use this much water!"

Graham chuckled and shook his head. "This water isn't meant for drinking. It has a solution in it to keep it clean. It's been here since Before Collapse and the original founders of the Mill decided to keep it. Not only does it provide relief on a scorching day, but it enables us to teach the children how to swim."

"There's hardly any water left to swim in. It needs to be preserved for drinking," Nixie protested.

"Maybe," Graham nodded, "but it's an important skill to have. What if a child was out and found a water source, fell in, and couldn't get out because it was too deep? It could happen. The child would drown. By instructing them, we're teaching them how to survive in an unknown situation."

Nixie could see the logic, but her mind reeled at the thought of so much water being used for pleasure rather than utility. The children were laughing, though, and it was a rare sight for her. The children from her group smiled only on rare occasions, and Faulkner didn't like laughter. It meant laziness, he said. "How much water do you put in each day?"

"Oh, none. We only add water when the levels start to drop. Look," he said, pointing up toward a canopy. "This used to be military camo netting. We salvaged it at the barracks After Collapse and put it up. You'll notice it above some of the more heat-sensitive crops that thrive in shade. Putting it over the pool has several functions. It keeps the heat of the sun off the people to let them enjoy time outside, it keeps too much water from evaporating, and it keeps pests out of the pool."

Nixie looked around the large outdoor area. Not only were people lounging around the space under the nets, but plants were growing, too. She walked over to one and cupped the leaves. "Blueberries."

"Yes, we managed to grow them around the property. They seem to thrive the best here."

Above the pool on a ledge, just inside fencing but outside of the netting, four stately apple trees threw their shade over the pool.

"This is incredible."

"It took a long time, but we got it there. All of the ornamental plants were ripped up shortly After Collapse and were replaced with fruit- or nut-bearing species. The original Settlers wanted this place to be as efficient as possible."

Nixie stared at the tableau in awe. Nothing she could say would adequately describe how she felt, so she merely nodded. *There's so much going on here. So many* right *things are happening. How did I not know this?* What else had Faulkner been keeping from everyone all these years? He painted the Settlers as these terrible people, but so far she saw nothing but order and discipline, without the screaming and threats. Nixie stepped back into the recreation room and passed through. Graham hurried after her.

"Is everything okay?"

"Yes," she lied. "I just…it's a bit much."

"I can see how it could be. Let's go back up and get something to eat. Then I'll show you more of the compound."

As they entered the building, a young man with graying black hair skidded to a halt before them. His skin was an unhealthy shade of white. She'd never seen someone so pale before. He stared wide-eyed at Nixie, flicked his eyes up at Graham, and then back again. In his hands he held a crumpled piece of paper, which he thrust at her.

She jumped back, surprised.

"Have you seen these before?"

"Static, not now."

"But it's important. I'm so close, and Peyton won't let me talk to her. I just need a moment of your time," he said, his eyes darting nervously around as if to keep watch. He held out the paper, nearly pushing it into Nixie's hand as she reached out to take it. "I need these items. I'm rebuilding the radios. To make contact with the others. To reconnect. And I need these."

Nixie looked down at the paper, trying to smooth it out as best she could. She turned it one way, then the other. Some of the images were vague sketches, and others were much more detailed. "I'm sorry. I have no idea what these are."

Static let out a groan of frustration, closing his eyes. "I *need* them."

"I mean, I've seen old radios, but never things like this."

His eyes snapped open. "Old radios? Where?"

"Hartford. The big city from Before Collapse." She'd been sent on a mission into the city with Ranger and a few others. Faulkner thought maybe there'd be water in a tank somewhere. It had been pointless. She'd seen the hulks of abandoned buildings and stores that still had some items left that had been obsolete in After Collapse society.

"We have to go. We have to go! You can show me where," he shouted, grabbing her arm. Nixie let out a startled yell and Graham pulled Static off her.

"You're not going into the city," he snapped at the young man. "Not without clearance from Peyton and the others. Go bother them if you want to go on your fool's errand."

For the first time since their meeting, Static's eyes cleared and he stood straighter. His voice, seconds ago laced with hysteria, was calm and measured. "It's not foolish. I know what I'm doing. I'm going to get us reconnected. Just watch," he said, and his calm faded. He grabbed the paper from Nixie and disappeared around the corner. Nixie stared, speechless, at the spot he'd just left.

"Excuse him. Ever since he heard a Traveler talk about a rebuilt city down south he's spent too much time cooped up with his defunct electronics." Graham laughed, but to Nixie it sounded bitter. "If he'd been alive long Before Collapse, I'd say he was one of those teens addicted to their iPhones and computers. However he's hardly seen working tech, so I don't understand it." When she stared at him blankly he explained. "They were electronics, devices you could use to call people, play music, and watch cat videos."

"Cat videos?"

"Yeah. It's exactly like it sounds. Moving pictures of cats and their antics."

Nixie couldn't imagine anyone wasting time watching cats, but she left it alone. "How old is Static? In his forties?"

Graham shook his head. "No, he's only twenty-five."

"But his hair…"

"Is already starting to gray, I know. He never stops."

"Why do you think he spends too much time working on those things?" Nixie asked, genuinely curious about the strange young man. "I mean, if he wants to make contact with other people, isn't that good?"

"It sounds good, but there was another man before him who tried. He failed."

"So? Static might do it, right?"

Graham gave her a weary smile. "Maverick worked in communications Before Collapse. If anyone was going to get the radios working again, it was him."

"Well couldn't he help Static? Where is he now?"

"After working at it for years he just...gave up. He left the Mill one day about fifteen years ago. Disappeared. We sent people out to find him or his body, but nothing ever came up. None of the other settlements had seen him."

"Maybe he decided to, I don't know, travel somewhere else."

"He didn't take anything with him." Graham sighed. "How could he survive? I don't want to see that happen to Static, too."

CHAPTER TWELVE

Static's excitement was palpable as Peyton sat across from him at her desk. He would sit down for a moment, only to jump back out of his seat and pace. Ten steps, turn, ten steps back, sit. Repeat. "This is a huge breakthrough. Huge!" he said for the fifth time.

"You've said this before."

"I know, I'm sorry, I'm excited. I can't help it!"

"I'm not talking about today, Static. I mean other times we've brought you back equipment."

He ran his fingers through his hair, fisting the strands briefly before letting go. His already messy hair stood up even more, looking like a cow had taken a tongue to it. The image had Peyton biting back a laugh. She covered her mouth with a hand to keep it contained.

"This is different."

"How?"

"Because Nixie said she knew a place where there are still radios. I *know* I can get what I need there. I feel it." He stopped pacing and dropped back into the chair, clasping his hands together and forcing them between his knees to keep them still. "Please, Peyton. Give me a team and let me go. I won't ask again if what I need isn't there. I swear it."

"She could have just been saying things to make you leave her alone, you know." Barely a week into her stay and Nixie was already stirring up trouble—and with Static, of all people.

"I don't think she was."

"How does she know for sure?"

"Get her in here and ask her. Please, Peyton. I'm begging you. That Traveler said—"

"I know what the Traveler said, but they tell stories for food and shelter. You can't trust what they say."

"But he had *details* that he couldn't possibly know unless—"

"Unless he lived when everything worked. Static, not everyone has forgotten what it was like Before."

Static hung his head and sighed.

What harm would it do, really, to humor him this one time? If it got him off her back for a while, then really it was a win-win situation. Peyton scratched at her cheek and glanced at the papers in front of her. The only problems were time and manpower.

"What city?" she finally asked. His eyes lit up and Peyton held up a hand to stop him. "Don't get excited. I'm just trying to figure out the logistics *if* we were to take a trip like this. We can't just leave tomorrow, you know."

"I know," he said, nodding enthusiastically. He looked like an old doll Dad had found on one of his routes, whose head wobbled around loosely on a spring. A bobble-head, he'd called it. "Hartford. She said it was Hartford."

Peyton spun her chair around and stared at the maps on the wall behind her, with routes outlined in various colors for their different purposes. To the far left she found the map of Hartford and bit her lip.

"No one's gone there in years. We don't even have any clear routes into the city." She frowned. There were bridges, but they could have deteriorated over the years. Turning back to Static she sighed. "Give me a few days. I'll see what I can do about mapping out a route and getting together a group of people."

Static exploded out of his seat. "Thank you! Peyton, you're the best."

"I know."

He came around her desk, nearly tripping as he did, and pulled her out of her chair into a fierce hug.

Startled, Peyton kept her arms at her sides for a moment before tentatively reaching up to lightly hug him.

"I promise I'm going to get us reconnected to people who have already rebuilt."

Peyton hesitated before speaking softly. "If anyone can, it'll be you." *At least, now that Maverick's gone,* she amended to herself.

"I swear I won't bother you until you make your decision. You won't hear a word from me."

"Somehow I highly doubt that."

Static skipped from the office and ran into Graham in the doorway. He muttered an apology and then disappeared around a corner.

Graham came into the office with one eyebrow raised and Peyton sighed.

"I take it you caved?"

"I told him to give me a few days to look into it. He swore he'd never ask again."

Graham laughed and dropped into the seat Static had just vacated. "Yeah, that'll happen. Do you really believe what that Traveler told us?"

Peyton rubbed her forehead, her head aching just a little. "Not really, no. But I guess…maybe it's a possibility."

"Static is starting to rub off on you."

Peyton changed the subject. "Where's Nixie?"

"She's with Avery, getting some clothing. She seemed pretty excited about Avery's baby. They took to each other immediately. And before you panic, Julian is there. If I hover too much, she'll know something is going on."

Peyton nodded, the question on her lips fading. She should have known to trust Graham to make the right decisions. "That's good that she's getting along with someone else."

"Is it? What are your intentions, exactly?"

What were her intentions? Conversion? Make her life comfortable so she'd never want to leave the Mill? It was one more mouth to feed, but also another pair of hands to help with the work. A pair of slim, dainty hands that seemed strangely pale given her lifestyle. She frowned and pulled the map of Hartford carefully from the wall. No point in thinking about her. She was a Scavenger, even if she was beautiful in a delicate way.

Back to Graham she cleared her throat and fought the flush she felt creeping up her face. "Have you ever been to Hartford?"

"Before? Yes. After? A few times. I was with your father the last time we went into the city."

"What are the chances we'll find what Static needs?" she asked, sitting back in her chair, leaving the map between them.

Graham rubbed his chin thoughtfully, his eyes unfocused. "To be honest," he said after a few moments' hesitation, "I don't know. Since he's looking for electronics, specifically radio equipment, he might have an easier time. I don't think we went into the place he's looking for."

"You wouldn't happen to know the name of it, would you?"

"Actually, yes. I'm pretty sure she's talking about RadioShack. Where it is, I wouldn't know. But I think there was one in Hartford Before. Considering priorities were medicine, food, and clothing, in that order, the odds are fair something is still there. Riots were common in the beginning and people did steal a lot of the more expensive technology, but RadioShack didn't carry lots of inventory in-store. It might have been overlooked."

"Will it have what he's looking for?"

"That's a risk you're going to take if you're set on doing this."

Peyton sighed and leaned back in the chair, looking up at the ceiling above her. Here and there, knots in the original beams stared down at her like eyes, watching her as she struggled to make her decisions. "What would Dad have done?"

Graham chuckled. "He would have seen it as an adventure. But you're not your father. Make your decisions based on what *you* feel is right, not on what he would have done."

"Sometimes I think it would be easier if I just did everything the way he did."

"You can't do that. First of all, you're not him. People don't look at you the same way they looked to your father. Yes, you're his daughter, but it's not the same. Second, I know you questioned some of the things he did. Even when he was alive, you wanted to do things differently, and now you have your chance."

"I don't want that chance."

"I know. We've gone over this before, but now it's yours. Whatever you decide, I know you'd make him proud."

Tears welled in Peyton's eyes and she spun the chair to stare at the maps again. She'd make Dad proud and avenge his death. It wouldn't bring him back, but it was all she could do. "Would you be able to recommend a route to take?"

"Of course, but you may have to adjust it."

"The bridges."

"Yeah, they might be down. Even if they are, given the water shortage, the river might be passable. We haven't been down there in so long. Last time we went into the city, the water levels were lower than Before."

"The trip could serve two purposes. Satisfying Static and giving us a new water source." She turned once her eyes had cleared to see Graham making a face.

"Possibly, but there're two problems with that."

"What?"

"The distance and pollution."

Peyton laughed. "You think there's still pollution in a free-flowing river? Even so long After?" When Graham didn't respond she thought about the sources they had found in abandoned neighborhoods. "Oh."

"Right. Take a test kit and check it out. Couldn't hurt."

Changing topics, she pushed the map to the side and asked, "Should I take Nixie with me?"

"Your decision who you take, but I think she could help you. She might be the only one to remember where the store is."

"I'd take Jasper."

"Not Ryan?" Graham asked, eyes widening. "I'd have thought you'd want to keep him under your thumb."

"I'd rather do that, but he doesn't get along with Static and he hates Nixie. He'd be more trouble than it's worth. If he stays here, Willow and Julian can keep an eye on him."

Graham's lips tilted up in a smile. "That, my dear child, is exactly how your father would think."

CHAPTER THIRTEEN

A very hummed as she held up a dress to Nixie's slim frame, smiling brightly. "This will fit perfectly, and the colors will look wonderful on you."

"Dresses are a bit impractical, don't you think?" Nixie asked, holding her arms out. She felt like a doll being dressed up, but Avery seemed to be having a good time and she didn't want to upset a woman so pregnant she looked like she might go into labor if she sneezed.

"Sometimes, yes, but if you're staying in the Mill, they're nice. Besides, they're a lot cooler than wearing pants," Avery said with a wink. She placed it in the pile beside her. "At least take the one."

Nixie laughed. "Okay, fine. Just that one."

Avery placed a hand on her belly, pressing gently.

"Are you okay? Are you going to have the baby now?" Nixie asked for the fifth time since meeting the woman.

"No, I'm fine." Avery giggled. "I still have a few weeks to go, believe it or not."

She didn't look annoyed at all the questions. Instead, her face looked patient. She was going to be a great mother, Nixie thought. "What do you think you'll have?"

"I don't know." She pulled another shirt from the drawer, placing it to the side when she read the tag, and leaned back in for another. "I'll be happy with either, but I do hope I have a little girl."

"What does Julian want?"

"A boy." They both laughed.

Avery couldn't be much older than her, yet Nixie felt a strong connection with her. It wasn't motherly, though the young woman radiated a motherly vibe. It was something else. Sisterly, perhaps. Nixie had always wanted a sibling. She had often wondered what that would be like when her mother was still alive. At night she would watch the other children in the camp playing or squabbling with their brothers and sisters, and she'd envied them. She wanted someone to play with, to fall asleep with at night. Once she had even asked her mother why she didn't have any brothers or sisters, but her mother had never answered her question. *Maybe she couldn't have any more after me*, she thought.

"Do you have any names picked out?" Nixie asked, pulling out a shirt and holding it up to her. Avery gave her a thumbs-up and she put it in the pile she was taking.

"We've thought of a few, but we'll decide once we see the baby. I like Kate for a girl, but Julian likes Jasmine. He likes Darien for a boy, but I like David."

"At least the boy names both start with the same letter." Nixie smiled.

"That's true! But we'll see. Who knows? Maybe once the baby is born, none of those names will fit and we'll have a baby named Agamemnon!"

The idea of a little baby with such a long, crazy name struck Nixie, and she burst out laughing, quickly doubling over. Avery couldn't contain her own giggles and was soon lying back on the bed, out of breath.

Julian came into the room, eyeing them both. "What's so funny?"

"Nothing," Avery managed, waving her hand. "Just a little girl talk."

Julian raised an eyebrow and then sighed, turning back the way he came. "Get two women together and there's nothing but gossip," he teased.

Avery stuck her tongue out, though he couldn't see it, and pushed herself back up to a sitting position.

"Were you matched together?" Nixie asked, lifting the drawers they had sorted through and putting them back into the large dresser at the foot of the bed.

"Matched? No, of course not. Why do you ask?"

"Isn't that how everyone is paired off? Your leader matches you with someone?"

"No, not at all. Is that how things are done with the Sca—with your people?"

Nixie dropped to the floor by Avery's feet and nodded. "Of course. That's how it's always been. The one in charge makes all the decisions."

"That sounds silly to me. Who would know best who belongs together but the people involved?" Avery asked.

Nixie said nothing.

"Julian and I were friends as children, and as we grew up, we fell in love. It just seemed natural to be with him."

"So you made the decision?" Nixie asked, marveling when Avery nodded an affirmative. Yet another thing that differed between her people and the Settlers. "When two people are old enough, Faulkner makes the decision."

"Faulkner is your leader?"

"Yes. He...well he wants the best for us." At least, that's what she'd grown up believing. But why couldn't they decide who they wanted to be with? Avery was right. *And what if I don't want to be with a man? Faulkner can't force me.*

"Sometimes those who think they know what's best for us don't really," Avery said gently. She pushed herself up from the bed and picked up a pile of the clothing. "Let's bring this back to your place."

"Oh! I can get that." Nixie popped up, taking the pile from Avery and adding it to those she'd left behind. She followed the woman out of the apartment.

They lived on the third floor, so Nixie followed her up the steep stairs to the fourth floor. It took Avery some time to get up them, and Nixie briefly wondered if she should be doing it, but Avery insisted she was fine. By the time she got to the top floor she breathed a little heavier, but then, so did Nixie. She was not used to stairs of any sort. "Thank you, Avery. I appreciate what you've done for me."

"What, letting you borrow clothes?" She laughed. "It's nothing! They don't fit me anymore, so what's the point of holding on to them."

"But once you have the baby you'll need them."

"Not for a while. Besides, you need them now." Avery opened the door to Graham's apartment and Nixie followed her in, stunned. These people shared their resources. They worked together to make their lives better. They even had forms of recreation that her people couldn't begin to imagine.

Why hadn't she seen through Faulkner's self-serving lies before? If she had, if they all had, perhaps Enrique wouldn't have had to die...

Four days out of Dr. Easton's care and Nixie was already making herself useful. Peyton watched from the second-floor window of her office as Nixie followed Graham and two other foragers back into the complex. She was talking animatedly, with her hands waving, and Graham had a fond look on his face. Clearly, she'd already worked her way into his heart. Not that it was hard to do—with Graham, anyway. Peyton had to admit the girl had her charms. She was incredibly petite, barely clearing Peyton's shoulders, which had to put her at just above five feet, if that. And if her diminutive stature wasn't distracting enough, once Dr. Easton had cleaned her up and she'd put on Avery's clothing, she was downright beautiful.

Pity she was a Scavenger.

Peyton continued to watch their progress across the courtyard when Nixie looked up at the very window she stood in. Peyton didn't have enough time to duck out of the way. The Scavenger paused before waving. Without thinking about what she was doing, Peyton lifted her hand in a wave.

"Have you heard a single word I said?" Willow asked from her seat.

Peyton cringed inwardly and turned from the window to see her friend lounging in her own chair rather than the one for visitors. "Sorry, I was distracted."

"I couldn't tell," she said with a roll of her eyes. "Who were you waving at?" When Peyton didn't answer fast enough, Willow jumped up and peered out the window herself. She gasped. "The Scavenger? Seriously? You've got it bad."

"What have I got bad?"

"Don't play dumb. You like her."

Peyton snorted. There was no way she liked her. Okay, so maybe she had been thinking about how beautiful she was before Willow interrupted her, but that didn't mean she *liked* her. She could simply appreciate beauty where she saw it. "Get back to work."

"I've been trying to. Anyway, the reports are in from last night. Julian said someone tried to get into the building. He and Bill were on their rounds and they heard noise by that storeroom. You know, the one they first broke into."

That got Peyton's attention. "Did they see who it was?"

"No, but Julian is sure it's the same people as before. I mean, what are the odds of them targeting that same place?"

"Do you think they didn't get whatever it was they were after?"

"It's possible. Or they came back for the girl."

Peyton frowned.

"You're not going to tell her, are you?"

Would she tell her? No. What was the point? They were just getting her settled in. News of last night's break-in attempt would remain with those who ran the Mill, and regardless of how well she seemed to be fitting in, Nixie wasn't one of them.

❖

"I want to go with you into the city," Nixie said from Peyton's doorway.

The young guard looked up at her, eyes widening. "You what?"

"You heard me. I can help. I'm pretty sure I could lead you back to the place."

Peyton pushed aside what she had been working on and folded her hands on the desk. "I haven't even decided whether or not we're going."

"You will. I talked to Static yesterday, and I know I can help."

Peyton sighed and pinched the bridge of her nose with two fingers. Nixie stepped into the room, taking a seat without being invited. Peyton's long hair had escaped its ponytail, and the disheveled look suited her. It made her look softer somehow, approachable. Nixie tried to ignore the feelings it stirred in her stomach as she shifted in the uncomfortable folding chair.

"I could kill him," Peyton said after a few moments of silence.

"If it helps any, he didn't come talk to me. I talked to him. He seems so sure that it will work, and well, I want to be of some help."

"Why?"

Nixie looked down at her hands. She'd folded them in her lap, fingers twisted together. "I want you to be able to trust me." She needed to get back to her people, to tell Ranger what she'd learned. It was clear now that Faulkner needed to be replaced, and the only one strong enough to do it was Ranger. She could ask Peyton to let her leave, but she doubted the girl would be so willing to just let her walk away. Maybe, if her own people hadn't killed Peyton's father, she would have. But now, Nixie knew she had to further prove herself.

Or create the opportunity.

"Again, why?" Peyton asked, pulling her from her musing. "You've only been here, what, two weeks now? Why would you want to help Static?"

"He's different. Like me."

"Static has been with us since…well, for as long as I can remember."

"Yes," Nixie said leaning back in the chair. "And everyone ignores him. He doesn't have a role here, not a real one. Just like me."

Peyton barked out a short, almost-bitter laugh. "The situation is hardly the same. His job is to work on his radios. He doesn't do well with anything else, trust me. He can't concentrate enough to be useful. He almost got himself killed as a hunter. He nearly killed everyone else when he picked water hemlock instead of wild carrots during his stint as a forager. And as a guard?" She snorted and Nixie could only imagine what he'd done.

"How can he do his job at all if he doesn't have the right equipment?"

"The radios are unfixable, Nixie. Far more experienced people have tried—"

"Maverick," Nixie interjected.

Peyton pierced her with a questioning stare.

"Graham told me," she said. "And Static may not be Maverick, but who's to say his instincts are wrong? If he's right and he fixes the radios, he will prove himself useful, right? If he doesn't, you'll be no worse off. So let me help. Just let Static try. It can't hurt." Nixie didn't give her the time to say anything. She just stood and walked back across the room to the door. She had almost passed completely through when she looked back over her shoulder. "By the way, Graham wants you to eat dinner with us tonight." She smiled. "He said something about you not eating right." As she retreated, she heard a faint laugh, and her smile widened.

Maybe the big, tough guard wasn't so tough after all.

CHAPTER FOURTEEN

When Nixie opened the door rather than Graham, Peyton was thrown off for a moment, and she nearly turned back with an apology before Graham walked by in the background, carrying a casserole dish.

"Graham just finished making dinner," Nixie told her as she opened the door wider to admit her. Peyton could only nod in response and step across the threshold.

It wasn't seeing Nixie there that threw her off. Not really. It was seeing her in the flowing, soft coral dress that fell just short of her knees. Tongue-tied, Peyton blurted, "Why are you wearing a dress?" and then bit the inside of her cheek before she said anything else ridiculous. *What the hell is wrong with me?*

Nixie looked down before twirling. "Avery pretty much demanded I take it, and I didn't want to disappoint her." A faint blush colored her cheeks, mirroring what Peyton was sure colored her own—although, if the burning in her face was any indication, hers was about ten shades brighter. "What was wrong with what you were wearing before?" Peyton asked, and then winced. *You are not allowed to talk the rest of the night.* She wanted to curse herself for being so blunt.

Graham came to her rescue—sort of—at that moment. "I suggested she wear it tonight. A sort of formal dinner party. I should have told you to dress up, too."

Peyton glanced down at her patched jeans and faded T-shirt before she regained her composure and rolled her eyes. "As if I have anything fancy like that."

"Well, it's the thought that counts," he said and gestured toward the table. "Let's eat before everything gets cold."

Sitting at Graham's table for the first time since Dad's death felt strange, especially with Nixie sitting in what used to be his favorite seat, right by the window. Every so often he would glance out to see what was happening, and Nixie did the same thing. After Nixie's third glance out the window, she caught Peyton staring. "Do I have something on my face?" she asked, reaching up to wipe it away.

Peyton shook her head. "No, sorry." She paused, dismissing several excuses in an instant before deciding to be honest. "Just thinking about my dad. He used to sit there." The slow burn of anger over his senseless death bloomed in her chest, like reopening a wound. She struggled to push it away. She wanted to enjoy her dinner tonight.

Nixie looked down at her hands. "I'm sorry."

"Don't be. It's not like you did it." Peyton turned away from Nixie to look at the spread before them. Graham had put together a simple casserole with zucchini noodles, tomatoes, peppers, and other vegetables either grown on the farms or foraged. The food was something she was familiar with. Graham had called it comfort food before, and she supposed it was that.

Nixie carefully scooped some of the casserole onto her fork, looking at it for a moment, before carefully, almost reverently lifting the fork to her mouth. Her lips closed around the food slowly, and as soon as they did, her eyes slipped shut. She even chewed slowly, taking her time with each bite, as if savoring it. Watching Nixie eat was like watching the ground soak up the water during a gentle rainstorm. Peyton realized she was staring again, but she'd never seen a person eat like that before, as if each bite was the best thing she'd ever tasted.

Under the table, Graham kicked her and she let out a low grunt. She tossed him a glare, and when she looked back at Nixie, the girl was watching her.

"Graham's a pretty good cook, so you're lucky you're staying with him," Peyton managed, taking quick bites and filling her mouth with food so she wouldn't have to speak.

Nixie nodded. "He is. We don't have anything like this at my camp. It's so basic." She frowned and put her fork down.

"What's wrong?" Despite having a mouthful of food, she spoke around it anyway, earning her a sigh from Graham. She flashed him a look of apology.

"Nothing, really," Nixie said. "It's just...every time I eat a meal here, I think of how little we have. The food here is like art. Everything is special."

Peyton swallowed her food and laughed. "It's just a casserole. I hated them as a kid. It was practically all Dad could make."

"Peyton," Graham warned. But of what, she couldn't tell.

She took another bite of her food and waved the fork, gesturing toward the dish. "What? It's true. It's like, the easiest dish someone can make. You take out a bunch of crap, throw it together, and you have food."

Nixie shoved back her chair and stood abruptly. "Just a bunch of crap? It's that easy? It would be, for a Settler like you," she spat. "When you have working ovens and electricity. We don't have that luxury."

Peyton stared at her, mouth open at the fire in her eyes.

"You take everything you have for granted. You don't have to struggle for anything. And you think you're all better than us?" Nixie laughed, but it was full of venom rather than humor. "You're nothing but a bunch of pampered, self-absorbed, selfish—"

"Nixie, that's enough." Graham cut her off calmly, not even looking up from his meal. Peyton gaped at him as Nixie listened. She turned, excused herself, and stormed out of the room. Footsteps thundered on the stairs and reminded Peyton of her own angry outbursts when she was a child.

Something about that memory made her want to laugh, but the look on Graham's face cut it short. "What?" she asked. "You heard what she called us. Why didn't you say something?"

"She's right."

"Excuse me?"

"We are pampered. We certainly have more than her people do. We should be grateful."

"You're joking. Come on, Graham! They could have it, too, but they stay out there and steal."

"Maybe some do, but we don't know all of the circumstances, do we?"

"So now you side with the Scavengers? The people who killed Dad?"

"That's not it." He paused, then said, "Having her stay with me has been an enlightening experience. We've learned a lot from each other. Maybe it's time for you to learn from her, too."

Peyton scoffed at the idea, but without much passion behind it. Why had she picked a fight? It could've been a nice evening with good food and good company, but something triggered her. The more she replayed it, the worse she felt. As Graham finished his last bite of the casserole and picked up both his dish and hers—even though she wasn't finished—she hung her head and sighed. "Okay, fine. What should I do?"

"What a normal human being would do. *Talk* to her."

A knock on Nixie's doorframe alerted her to the presence she couldn't see. Since she hadn't heard Graham's heavy footsteps on the stairs, she knew it could only be one other person.

"Go away," she said into her pillow. Funny how she had already started to consider this room as hers, even though everything was borrowed and her stay temporary.

"I want to talk to you."

"Well, I don't want to talk to you."

Peyton laughed, and not the cruel laugh like at the table, but one of pure amusement. "You sound like Jasper when he's upset with me or Willow."

"So people being upset with you is a common event, then?"

A moment of hesitation. "You could say that."

Footsteps creaked on the floor in her room but stopped once they reached the center. She turned her head to stare at the white walls. "If you're here because Graham told you to talk to me, then just go. It's a waste of our time."

"I know, but I'm off for the rest of the evening and he knows it. So I guess I have to stay here for a little while at least. Make it *seem* like we're patching things up."

"Then I guess you'd better sit or something."

Footsteps and a creak as Peyton settled into a patched-up chair in the corner of the room. "I have to say, your exit wasn't bad. You get points for style."

Nixie reluctantly sat up and turned to look at her. "It felt kind of nice to storm away to my room. I never had my own room."

"Never?"

She shook her head and found herself talking, even though she was still angry. "We have…tents, sort of, but we share them as families. I shared one with my mother."

"Tents aren't that bad. We use them when we go out for days at a time."

"Try living in one permanently."

A pause. "You said your mother died, so don't you have your own tent now?"

"It's not really the same as having my own space. My shelter is open to most of the others. It's hard to describe." She struggled to put the words together, to make Peyton understand. "You have walls. Solid walls. We don't. So even when we're separated, we're together. I may not be able to see everyone else, but I can hear everything they do, and sometimes that's just even more invasive than seeing."

Peyton frowned, leaning over and resting her elbows on her knees. She rubbed her hands together, back and forth. The slide of her palms made a soft rustling sound. "I guess that could be rough. I like my privacy."

"I hardly know what that is."

Silence lapsed between them, but the tension disappeared. Nixie felt oddly at ease with Peyton in her room, even though she'd been furious with her moments before. Even if she did make ignorant comments, she was at least trying, right? Nixie swung her legs off the edge of the bed. "You know, before this I'd never slept on a mattress."

"Seriously? What do you sleep on?"

Nixie shrugged. "Whatever we can scavenge." She smiled, but there wasn't much joy in it. "Guess that's why you call us Scavengers, huh?"

"Look, maybe I was wrong. A bit," Peyton said, hanging her head. Her eyes focused on the ground and even when Nixie stood, her eyes never wavered.

"About what?"

"About you. Some of you. I mean, you can't be all bad, right?" She jerked her head up and winced. "I'm sorry, that came out so wrong. Let me try that again. Whatever you were doing here, you had your reasons. You're just trying to survive. Our people just have different methods."

Nixie nodded. "You could call it that."

"You still shouldn't have stolen it though, whatever it was," Peyton said, but her tone was different this time. Before it had been accusing, and this time Nixie didn't detect that earlier edge.

"We don't steal because we're bad people, Peyton. We have no other choice. When you're desperate..." She offered a weak shrug. "My people need help."

Peyton stared at her for a moment and the look was so intense Nixie wondered if she could see her deepest secrets, wondered if Peyton knew she had been there when her father was killed. She had to look away and cross her arms over her chest to hold in the weight of the horrible secret. After what felt like minutes, but could only have been seconds, Peyton spoke up. "When we get back from Static's trip, maybe I can talk to the others. Maybe there's something we can do for your people."

Nixie whipped her head around to stare, wide-eyed. "Really?" She narrowed her eyes just as quickly. "Is this a trick?"

Peyton laughed and the pleasant sound sent a wave of chills down Nixie's spine, the sensation not dissimilar to the tingles she felt when a heavy rainstorm approached.

"No trick"—Peyton held out her hand—"I swear."

Cautiously Nixie took it. Peyton's hand was rough from work and larger than her own. When their fingers closed and gripped, Peyton's eyes flew open.

A wave of warmth flowed up Nixie's arm and she involuntarily shut her eyes, lips parting slightly as goose bumps broke out over her skin.

What the hell?

What is this all about?

Their hands lingered much longer than necessary, but Nixie didn't want to lose that contact. In the end, Peyton pulled her hand away first and Nixie was left with the loss of warmth. When she opened her eyes again, Peyton's face, which she kept turned to the floor, glowed pink.

"So," Peyton said, clearing her throat. "Truce?"

"Truce."

CHAPTER FIFTEEN

Peyton surveyed the group before her with their packs of gear. It had taken nearly two weeks after she made her decision to rearrange schedules and get everything settled, but she'd made it work, and she was confident they'd only be gone three days. With Willow and Julian in charge, plus Graham backing them, Ryan would hardly have time to breathe, let alone cause trouble.

Dawn had just broken and light filtered softly through the trees, giving everything a dreamlike quality. Static was quiet, but he bounced on his toes, fingers clenching the straps of his backpack. Jasper had his fingers laced behind his head, stretching his legs and back as he yawned. He kept his eyes closed, barely awake, and knowing him, he probably hadn't been awake for too long. A tuft of blond hair stuck up at an awkward angle and when he absently reached up to smooth it down, it just bounced back up. One of the foragers had decided to join them at the last minute, wanting to use the trip to update routes and mark new places on the maps. Cooper crouched near Jasper, rummaging through his packs, making sure he had everything he would need.

Nixie sat on a bench, her pack beside her. She looked calm, almost sleeping, as she stared up at the sky. It was hard for Peyton to tear her eyes from her. Since that moment in Nixie's room when they shook hands, something had changed between them. Peyton struggled to identify it, but the words eluded her. The antagonistic feelings she'd sometimes experience around the girl had disappeared. She admired her, in a way, but that wasn't the feeling. When they weren't together, every time she caught a glimpse of her, her pulse raced and her hands grew sweaty. She'd never had that problem before. She'd even gone to Dr. Easton to make sure she wasn't getting sick, but the doctor had just laughed and sent her on her way. And when they were together, planning this trip and mapping out where in the city Nixie had been to eliminate as much travel time as possible, she often found herself staring at the Scavenger, unable to keep her eyes off her. She couldn't deny the girl was beautiful, especially when her eyes flashed in anger and her brows pulled down. Peyton had noticed, when Nixie concentrated, a wrinkle appeared between her eyebrows. Peyton didn't regret much in life; she didn't have time for it. But she did regret the way she'd treated Nixie during their first encounter and during the beginning of her stay. Yeah, she shouldn't have stolen from them, but she was undeniably nice. She wasn't what Peyton had thought a Scavenger would be.

Tearing herself from her thoughts, she stood up straight. "Everyone ready? We should move out. We need to make good time if we're going to make it back in three days."

Cooper stood up and shouldered his bag. "We'll be fine," he said as he buckled the straps across his chest and hips. He tightened the straps and Jasper glanced at him out of the corner of his eye.

Nixie stood and shouldered her own bag, adjusting it as Static turned, ready to march out. He continued to bounce on his toes.

Peyton rolled her eyes. She sure as hell hoped they had enough food to fuel his nervous energy, or he'd crash.

"I've got the route memorized, let's go!" he shouted.

Jasper yawned for the twelfth time. "Keep your voice down. People are still sleeping."

"Static, lead the way." Peyton jumped in to keep the peace. The last thing she needed was an argument before they even left the grounds.

The group fell in step behind Static as he took off at a brisk pace. Jasper and Cooper walked side by side behind him, followed by Nixie. Peyton brought up the rear, constantly scanning the surroundings as she went. It wasn't as if she expected danger, but she'd been trained to be hypervigilant, especially when away from the Mill.

After trudging up the hill and taking one of the side streets beyond the Mill grounds, Nixie fell back to walk with Peyton, and her heart thumped wildly in her chest. Peyton drew in a deep breath to try to calm it. *It's the strain from walking up the hill, that's all.*

Nixie breathed just as heavily and wiped her brow. "I hope it isn't all hill."

"Out of shape?" Peyton asked, trying to keep her voice light and teasing. "I'd have thought a Scavenger would be more fit than us."

Despite the crack at her background, Nixie laughed. The sound was high and breathless and her pace slowed momentarily. "I'm not used to carrying large packs around."

Peyton frowned. "But, as a forager, wouldn't you have to?"

Nixie grew silent. Peyton wasn't sure she'd answer and glanced at her, wondering what it was she'd said. She reviewed her words, but no—for once, she'd said nothing insulting.

"I didn't carry much because of my size," Nixie finally said, as they rounded a bend. An old stop sign tilted back on its post as if waving them ahead.

"Everyone pulls their weight at the Mill, size notwithstanding."

Nixie shrugged. "I did as I was told. Not my place to question things."

Peyton found that strange. Why wouldn't everyone pitch in and do their share of the work? If Nixie were a forager, she would have carried heavy packs. Unless she rarely found food, which would make her a bad forager...

"Hey, are we taking the roads the whole way?" Cooper asked. "Because that's cool and all, but if we do we're going to directly pass Ogden and the Ox Farm."

"What's wrong with that?" Jasper asked. "They know us. Won't be a problem."

"Yeah, but we got a Scavenger with us. You know how they feel about Scavs. No offense," Cooper added, with a nod toward Nixie.

"It's still early. They might not be out."

Static turned and walked backward, his fingers around the straps of his bag. "It's not like they'll know she's different unless you say something. She could be new." He turned back around and clipped the tip of his shoe on a chunk of gravel. He caught himself before he fell. "I'm okay!"

Peyton sighed. "Please tell me you have the first-aid kit," she murmured. Jasper turned and nodded with a grin.

"Packed extra, just in case."

"How would they know I'm not from the Mill?" Nixie asked.

"All of the nearby settlements are familiar with each other. We trade with them frequently, so over the years we've gotten to know each other well. Don't you know other groups of Scavengers?"

Again that noncommittal shrug. "Not really, no. I mean, we've met some of the leaders, but generally we don't mingle. It's too chaotic. Not safe. Best to just keep to ourselves."

"Wow." Peyton couldn't imagine not getting to know anyone from other areas. It seemed foolish. There were so many resources the others had access to. Why wouldn't they pool them and share?

"Things tend to go missing when two groups get together," she added quietly, her voice pitched low enough for only Peyton to hear. Before she could respond, Nixie continued. "How many other settlements do you trade with?"

The group slowed as they turned onto what used to be West Street and trudged up a less steep, but longer hill. Static finally slowed his pace and fell back with Cooper and Jasper.

"We do most of our trading with Ellington. It's just over a mile from us, and they're a large livestock farm. We get our meat from them. They don't have a doctor, so Dr. Easton trains their people in basic first aid and helps them out. We share maple syrup and honey, too. Ogden we'll pass in a bit. The houses were newly built with sustainable technology right before the Collapse, so most of the families that live there have been there since Before Collapse. We don't trade much with them, but we're friendly and share a wheat field. We found it easier to maintain that way."

"And the farm you mentioned?"

"It's a one-family deal. Ox Farm is another Before Collapse family that stayed put. They knew what they were doing and managed to thrive. A lot of the original settlers at the Mill worked their land to learn about farming before they got the land around the Mill under control. We probably wouldn't be here if it weren't for them."

"Are there any others?"

"Not around here. There are some farther out, probably a week or more of travel, but it's too far to trade with. We get some items through trade with Travelers, but it's usually not much. Most of the time we just give them a place to stay and some food in trade for their stories." She raised her voice. "And that's all most of them are. Stories." Static waved a hand, signaling that he'd heard her but had chosen to ignore it.

Nixie nodded. "We take them in, too. Listen to whatever news they bring from other groups."

The small group passed a field and a squat brick building surrounded by a high chain-link fence. "This is one of the wheat fields we share with Ogden."

"What about the brick building? Do you use that?"

Jasper turned around and stopped walking, butting into their conversation. "Yeah, it's perfect for meetings. It used to be some sort of barracks Before, or something like that. It goes deep—"

"Jasper," Peyton barked out his name harshly and he stopped talking. As much as Nixie was growing on her, she didn't want to reveal everything. Just in case.

Nixie looked at Jasper and he mouthed an apology. Peyton strode ahead to talk to Static. Nixie wanted to talk more but was grateful for the interruption. She knew this place well. She'd been with Ranger to these wheat fields once when he'd been sent out in the dead of night to harvest some of the ripened wheat. She'd thought nothing of it at the time, but now that she knew the people who relied on it, and that it belonged to multiple groups working together rather than just the one family who lived there, guilt tore at her stomach. Her people could just as easily learn to grow and harvest food rather than rely on stealing from others who did the work. She needed to get back to her people. They needed to know it could be different. Nixie felt energized, knowing she could be a force for changing things, making them better.

After I help Static find what he needs, I'll go back and find them. Teach them what I've learned.

She smiled at the thought. With a new purpose, she picked up her pace, keeping the smile in place as she matched her stride with Peyton's while Jasper dropped behind.

No one was out at the barracks, and when they crested the hill and started walking down, Ogden was quiet as well. They hadn't been walking long, and Nixie wondered if they would make it to Hartford faster than Peyton and the others anticipated.

"We should stop for water at Ox Farm. Fill up, just in case we don't run into any for a while," Cooper said as they passed a massive greenhouse.

Inside the gates of the property Nixie could hear shuffling, and as they passed trees, she saw dogs lying out on the ground. They spotted the group and growled, letting out a series of sharp barks. Two of the dogs ran toward them, and Nixie let out a short yell, jumping back behind Peyton.

The girl laughed, resting a hand on her shoulder. "Don't worry, they won't get you. They can't jump the fence. It's just to keep intruders out."

"We should probably pick up the pace, though," Jasper said, still coming up at the rear. "Don't want to piss off their owners by waking them early."

"Good call. Let's be quick about it then. We can stop for a rest at the farm."

CHAPTER SIXTEEN

The family at Ox Farm was already hard at work by the time Peyton and her group arrived. One of the youngest children sat on the steps of the wide porch holding a chicken. The rest of the hens clucked about at her feet, scratching the dirt.

Peyton held up a hand in greeting as they approached, stopping just inside the old paved driveway. "Is your mama around?"

The little girl nodded and turned her head before letting out a shrill, "Mama!"

Beside her, Nixie jumped. A young woman, just a few years older than Peyton, ran out of the farmhouse, eyes wide. "What's wrong?"

"People," the girl responded calmly and went back to her chickens.

"Sorry to trouble you so early, Mrs. Burgoine. We're heading into Hartford and were wondering if we could fill up our canteens."

"Oh! Peyton, of course. Come in. The way Ada was screaming I thought something had happened to her."

The group filed past the little girl onto the screened in porch. Mrs. Burgoine and Cooper brought the canteens in while the rest sat down on old wicker furniture.

"Mrs. Burgoine?" Nixie asked, raising an eyebrow.

"Some people still use last names," Static said, speaking for the first time since they left the Mill. "Those who stayed in the same area and didn't lose their families. Most of Ogden has last names."

"Do any of you?" Nixie asked, and they all shook their heads.

"Graham remembers his, but he doesn't use it. I can't remember what it is. Dad's was Gonzalez, but he stopped using it long before I came around."

Mrs. Burgoine reappeared on the porch with Cooper and passed the canteens around. "Cooper tells me you're looking for parts."

Static nodded. "I'm going to fix the radios and get us connected."

"Ah, so you're the infamous Static," she said with a smile. "Good luck. I hope you find what you're looking for."

"Thank you," Peyton said before Static could launch into an explanation. She could tell by the way his lips quirked he was ready to explain everything. "Is there anything we can pick up for you if we find it?"

"Actually, if you can manage it…if you spot any plastic bags."

"Of course," Peyton said.

"We have some netting we need to patch, and I've cleared out everything I can find in this area. I'm worried about our crops. Even with the netting some of them have started to burn. If things keep up, I don't know what we're going to do."

"We're having the same issues," Cooper said. "And some of the places we usually forage aren't yielding the amounts we need."

"Mushrooms seem to be nonexistent."

Before Cooper could continue on the finer points of mushroom cultivation, Peyton interrupted. "Thanks again, Mrs. Burgoine. We better be on our way."

"Anytime. Be safe."

The little girl waved at them as they left. The road before them stood open, and they traveled down what had once been a busy main street. On the sides stood the shells of the former police and fire departments. In the lot sat the remains of rusted vehicles. Once the fuel ran out, people stripped the machines of any potentially valuable parts. Anything that could be used was repurposed.

Before the sun even hit high noon, the group was exhausted and had depleted almost half their water. Despite milder temperatures that morning, it had turned into a scorcher. Peyton tried to keep them in the shade as much as possible and they plodded on slowly, but soon they approached the old highway and she faced a dilemma: at the rate they were going, they would definitely run out of water and they didn't even know if the river was still flowing. Time to brainstorm.

"Okay, we have a bit of a problem," Peyton said as she turned back to survey her group. They had stopped to rest under an old oak tree. Static lay in the grass, his face already red from the sun. Nixie fanned herself with her hand, sipping carefully on her canteen.

"What now?" Jasper groaned, his back to the tree. Beads of sweat trickled down his hairline and stained the collar of his shirt. "Don't tell me we forgot something."

"Not that. I had planned on taking the highway straight into Hartford. Navigating it will be easy—the deterioration won't be as extreme as the rest of the surface roads. It would get us there faster, but—"

"But we'll need more water, and there won't be a water source on the highway," Cooper finished.

Peyton nodded. "Exactly. We can stick as close to the highway as possible and stay in the trees, and that will give us a better chance of finding water to replenish our supplies."

"That will take longer, and we might run into Scavengers," Cooper said. He stared up at the leaves above him. "I say we take the risk and stick to the trees. Look at Static. He's already burning. Much more and he'll have heatstroke."

"I can make it," Static argued, but Jasper shushed him and made him lie back down.

Peyton looked to Nixie. "Do you know of any Scavenger groups in this area?"

Nixie shook her head. "Not this way, at least none that Faulkner is aware of. When I was out…foraging…we never came across any. It could have changed, so I can't guarantee it."

The strange hesitation in her reply threw up a red flag in Peyton's mind. When she said foraging, did she really mean stealing? She tried to quell the thoughts, but once on the surface they bubbled there, refusing to go away. She wanted to trust her, but her gut said to keep a cautious eye on her.

"Okay," she said, addressing the rest of the group. "We stick to the sides then. Hopefully we find a water source. Look for the signs, and speak up if you see anything."

Together they hauled Static to his feet and changed routes. Peyton led them down into the tree line that ran parallel to the old highway. Though the path wasn't straight or clear of debris, they picked their way carefully around obstacles and still made good time. By the time the sun hit its peak, everyone was dragging even more than before. Peyton worried about taking too many breaks. She hadn't planned for so many, but without them, they might be pushing themselves more than was wise. They'd reached Manchester by that point and were close to the old mall. A thick stand of trees ahead of them looked perfect for resting.

"We'll stop there for an hour," she said.

Static sighed with relief. He'd been dragging. His initial burst of energy had cut off hours earlier, and the rest of the group had slowed down to keep pace with him. When they reached the stand, he collapsed under a tree.

"Drink your water," Peyton insisted, picking up the canteen he'd dropped.

He reached out and took it, his eyes half-closed. His face was a startling shade of red, his hair looked as if he'd dunked his head in water, and sweat drenched his shirt. Peyton frowned. He had already burned in the sun despite their time under the trees.

"Jasper, give Static two tablets and make sure he eats something. Static, while we're in the shade, take your shirt off and relax."

Nixie sidled up to her, her eyes wide. "Is he going to be okay?"

Peyton offered her a small smile. "He never goes outside. We should have taken extra sun precautions for him but I didn't think—" She cut herself off with a curse and stared at the ground. "Dad wouldn't have made this mistake."

Nixie rested a small hand on her arm, squeezing lightly. A shock at the touch raced through Peyton's body and she suppressed a shiver despite the heat. Her mind supplied her with images of Nixie's exposed skin and she shook her head to clear it. Now was definitely not the time. Nixie was trying to talk to her. "We all make mistakes, right?"

"Not when you're supposed to be in charge, because those mistakes can hurt people."

"Hey. You're doing the best you can, we know that," Nixie said.

Peyton looked down at her and saw a look of genuine concern and something else, something she couldn't identify. "Thanks."

Nixie nodded without another word and took a seat by Static.

Peyton paced off to the side, away from everyone else, and pretended to look through her bag, but really she was looking at Nixie out of the corner of her eye. At some point the girl had gotten under her skin. She couldn't deny it—she was attracted to her. She wanted her. Part of her balked at the idea and didn't want to trust her. She was a Scavenger. The other part, the part that sounded suspiciously like her father, whispered to give Nixie a chance, because she could be trusted. Peyton really wanted to listen to that second voice…but at what cost?

Chapter Seventeen

Nixie sensed the water before everyone else. She breathed deeply, relishing the crisp, clean scent as it washed over her body. Her dry skin smoothed out, soaking in the moisture like a dying plant in a rainstorm. She couldn't tell if it was truly clean or not yet, but for now, just knowing water was nearby felt like a blessing. She didn't feel so lost anymore.

"We should be coming up on the river soon," Peyton said, confirming what Nixie already knew. She wanted to run toward it; her body practically screamed for it. Energy hummed within her, making it hard to concentrate.

"I'm so thirsty," Static gasped.

"Don't talk. Save your energy," Jasper said, standing at Static's side to support him if he dropped.

Nixie worried about him. Cooper had taken off his shirt and draped it over Static's head to shield him from the sun. His bronzed skin kept him protected from the strong rays—at least, more than Static's pale skin protected him. Static had also long since drained his water. She had given him sips from hers, urging him to drink slowly. If she needed to, she could try to regulate her own body, but there was so little moisture in the air. At least with a water source nearby, they could solve this one problem.

The sun had begun its descent in the sky, and though it was still light out, they would need time to find a place to sleep, set up shelter, and build a fire for the night. As they emerged from the wooded area by the highway, they were faced with a steep bank that led down to the river. Static let out a shout of joy, pulled away from Jasper, and stumbled down the hill.

"Static, wait!" Peyton called, running after him. The rest followed behind her, scrambling to remain upright.

The water level was incredibly low. Against the concrete pylons, the water level Before Collapse was clearly marked by dark lines. But what remained was hardly a trickle of the once wide river. Some of the ground that would have been underwater was now dried, with deep cracks on the surface.

It smelled strange. Nixie followed the group down, picking her way carefully so as not to slip on the rocks. She sniffed the air and immediately wrinkled her nose.

The water was tainted. What should have been a swiftly flowing river sat nearly stagnant before them. Her skin tightened as if to keep the dirty water from entering her body. But it was water, and it could be cleaned with filtration equipment and boiling. Bacteria floated invisibly in the murk, but they could make it safe with the right precautions, she was sure of it.

Just as she reached the river's edge, Static plunged his hands into the water and brought them up to his lips. Nixie screamed, "Stop! Don't drink it!"

Despite his thirst, Static froze and the water ran from his hands. "But it's water," he said, his voice quiet from her outburst.

"It's not safe. It needs to be cleaned. Filtered. Boiled." Peyton stared at her, and Nixie felt as if the guard could see into her mind. She glanced down at the water, trying to get away from those eyes.

"A little bit can't hurt," Peyton said. From the corner of her eye she could see Cooper nodding his agreement.

"Looks fine to me. It's clear. I don't see any rainbows indicating oil. It might not be the best idea, but just a sip or two can't kill him," he added.

When Nixie glanced at Static, he looked ready to cry. His hands twitched, his fingers glistening from the water they had once held.

"It's not safe," she repeated.

"How do you know?" Peyton's voice had gone cold, and Nixie felt the chill. How could she explain what she knew without telling them about her ability? Would they understand? Would they even believe her? Part of her wanted to trust them and explain, but another part—with Faulkner's voice attached—warned her not to. They could take advantage of her, bring her back to the Mill and lock her up. Use her. She looked around, frantically seeking some reasonable explanation, when her eyes lit on the carcass of a dog.

"The dog." She gestured to it. "It could have died from the water."

"It could have died from something else entirely. Besides, it wouldn't happen that fast if it died from the water," Peyton countered smoothly.

"Maybe. But do you want to take that chance?"

Peyton's eyes bored into her, but she stood her ground and even managed to straighten her shoulders. She held the gaze. Peyton was the one to break it.

"Static, don't you dare drink the water."

He cried out in frustration.

"We'll set up camp at the top of the bank and build a fire. Once we get the fire going, we filter and boil the water."

Nixie breathed a sigh of relief as she climbed the hill with the others to help set up camp. She felt Peyton watching her, but she didn't turn to look back.

It wasn't the dead dog that had tipped Nixie off. Peyton wasn't an idiot. She'd yelled long before she could have seen the carcass at the water's edge. So how had she known? Peyton eyed her as she followed everyone to the top of the hill. She didn't turn around, but it didn't matter. Judging by the stiffness in her back, she was fully aware that Peyton had watched her go.

Once Nixie was out of sight, she turned back to the water. What had tipped her off? She leaned over a bit, extending the upper half of her body as far over the water as she dared without losing her balance, and breathed in deeply. No strange smell. Nothing unusual, anyway, for a low river. She looked out over the surface, scanning up and down the banks and as far across as she could see. Nothing out of the ordinary there, either. Did she have some sort of X-ray vision? Peyton crouched and looked closely at the water, but again, saw nothing weird. No little creatures wiggled around. She didn't see any mosquito larvae.

So what the hell made her yell at Static like that?

Sure, the water didn't move as swiftly as it once would have, and faster-moving water was preferable. But there were so many rivers just like this one that they'd encountered with no problems. *Does she know something she isn't telling us?* But wouldn't she have given something away long before reaching the river? She had seemed just as desperate to get to water as the rest of them. Maybe she was just overly cautious. Maybe something happened to one of her people, Peyton tried to rationalize.

Doubt pushed its way into the recesses of her mind, chanting, *Ask her. Trust her.* It sounded like her dad. That was ridiculous. What would she say to her? "So, Nixie, what was up with you yelling at Static for trying to drink the water? You got some kind of power or something?" Yeah, because that sounded rational. She snorted to herself and stood, rubbing her hands on her jeans. She had started to turn back toward their path when she stopped.

Power.

The word triggered a memory...

A few years ago a Traveler had passed through and told stories of people who could find water with just their senses. He said they had heightened awareness, like witches from the nineteenth century. Of course Peyton and everyone else had brushed it off as just another story they told for a meal and night's sleep.

But what if the Traveler's stories were true?

No. That was ridiculous. It was one thing for them to spin tales of rebuilt cities—something so very possible. Still, she fought to disbelieve those stories, despite wanting them to be true—or maybe because of that. It would crush her to find out they'd been fabricated simply to earn a place to sleep for a night, and she couldn't bear that. But powers? Ridiculous. She wasn't a child. Fairy tales were just make-believe and had no place in her world.

Still...

Peyton looked back up the hill where the others had the start of two tents set up—one for the girls and one for the boys, as if they were still little kids—and where Cooper was working on a fire. Small tendrils of smoke floated up as orange ribbons curled around the logs. They'd have clean water soon.

Tonight, while the boys were sleeping, Peyton would ask.

She'd make it casual and watch Nixie's reactions.

She couldn't go very far, after all, while they were stuck together in a tent.

CHAPTER EIGHTEEN

Cooper had to wrench the canteen away from Static to keep him from drinking too much water, too quickly. Nixie felt for him, she really did. It had to be terrible to be sunburned so badly on top of the dehydration. She wished Dr. Easton were with them, to help him.

Jasper had applied a nasty smelling salve to his face, gently smoothing it across his skin in a tender way Nixie hadn't realized he was capable of. If she hadn't seen them interacting before, she would have thought they were lovers and turned away, but she knew better. While Jasper tended to his burns, Cooper kept feeding him small sips from the canteen.

Peyton slipped behind her and sat on the ground, her shoulder brushing Nixie's as she moved. "We should probably stay here for a day, let him recover. I don't want to waste the time, but I worry about him."

"He probably won't let that happen," Nixie replied, trying not to focus on the heat radiating from Peyton.

"Probably not." She hesitated, opening her mouth to say something, then stopping.

Nixie turned toward her, tilting her head to the side.

"I worry I made the wrong decision."

"About what?"

"Taking on this ridiculous mission and bringing him with us. He's not built for this sort of thing."

"He wanted to do it. Besides, only he knows what he needs for the radios, right? Someone else would bring back the wrong thing and it would be a waste of time."

Why was Nixie trying to comfort her? Peyton shook her head. "I wonder if my dad would have made this mistake."

Every time she mentioned her father it felt like a stab in Nixie's chest. "People aren't perfect. No one is. I'm sure he made a lot of mistakes, too. No offense," she added quickly when Peyton shot her a look. If she kept bringing him up, Nixie would be compelled to spill the truth. And she didn't know how Peyton would react. She'd kept it a secret for too long to let it go casually now, but it was starting to feel wrong not to tell her. She gnawed on her lip as Peyton spoke.

"Yeah, but he wouldn't have done something like this. Taking someone who's such a high risk on a mission."

Jasper had finished putting the salve on Static and helped him get comfortable. He'd finally had enough water for the moment and Cooper stirred a pot of food over the fire to keep it from burning.

"Dinner will be ready in a few minutes," he announced quietly. "I saw some berry bushes a little farther up. I'm going to check them out before it gets too dark." He grabbed a collapsible basket from his bag. "Jazz, keep an eye on the food?"

Jasper nodded and took his place. "It's a good thing you came along, Nixie. We'd have been screwed if we drank that water."

Nixie ducked her head to hide the color she knew stained her cheeks and pretended to find something by her side that required her immediate attention. "I'm sure you would have stopped him anyway. I was just more vocal about it."

"I don't know," Jasper replied, stirring the pot. "I was pretty thirsty myself. I probably would have had a few sips, too."

"Thirst makes you do crazy things, I guess," Nixie replied. She was conscious of Peyton's eyes on her again, and she wanted to crawl away and hide. What if she had given away too much in that warning? Would they figure out her abilities? Could they? How many others like her were out there? She'd never met another, but that didn't mean she was unique. They could be hiding their talents just like she was, and she would never know. No one would.

Doubt crept into her mind again as Faulkner's voice berated her for even considering revealing herself. But he was wrong about everything else, wasn't he? He lied, and Nixie had seen firsthand just how easy their life could be if they changed their ways.

The voice began to fade.

"I think it's done," Jasper said after a moment, breaking the silence. He lifted the spoon from the pot and gave it a tentative lick. His lips pulled back into a grimace. "Ugh. Foragers might be able to find food, but they sure as shit can't cook it."

"I heard that," Cooper grumbled as he came back with his basket half-full of berries. "For that, you don't get dessert."

Jasper pouted. "That's no fair."

"It's what you deserve."

Peyton cracked a smile and glanced at Nixie. "Boys," she said simply with a shrug. "What are you gonna do?"

The sun faded from the sky and an amazing array of stars peeked out from the darkness while the moon shed ample light. Between that and the fire, Peyton could see everything in her surrounding area, even if it took on a muted, almost ghostly feel.

Cooper and Jasper had put Static to bed, spreading more of the salve over his burned skin and making sure he was comfortable. A combination of that, cool water, and medication had him feeling much better, and he swore he'd be ready to go in the morning. Peyton still hadn't decided whether or not they'd stay camped for another night. She'd check on him in the morning. No way was she going to push them and risk serious injury to one of the people under her care.

After sitting out by the fire, finishing the berries—of which Jasper stole a few handfuls—and chatting mindlessly for a while, the boys turned in for the night. Peyton had insisted on taking the first watch. Jasper had helped Static through the last few hours and she knew he had to be exhausted. Her instincts proved correct when he argued only once before crawling into the tent after Cooper.

"You should get some sleep, too," she told Nixie as the girl remained by her side.

Nixie shrugged. "It's a nice night out. I don't mind."

"I don't need the company." She realized how harsh that sounded after the words left her mouth and quickly backpedaled. "But I guess I wouldn't mind it." She was supposed to be finding out how she knew about the water.

The Scavenger smiled and poked at the fire with a long stick, stirring the flames. Sparks leapt from the makeshift pit. Logs hissed and popped, adding music to the night.

They sat in silence for some time while Peyton surveyed the land. Occasionally a dog barked in the distance or coyotes howled. After Collapse, animals moved back into territories that had been taken from them by humans. Dad had told her Mother Nature was restoring the balance.

"Do you believe in a sort of Earth spirit?" Peyton suddenly asked. The words surprised her, and she felt foolish for asking it, but Nixie didn't look at her strangely. In fact, she looked intrigued by the question. "Like a god?"

"No, not that. I don't know what I mean."

"I think I understand." Nixie set the stick down and rested her hands on her knees. "I don't know. I suppose there could be something. Why do you ask?"

"It's something my dad used to talk about sometimes. He thought one of the reasons society fell was because of how we treated the planet, and Mother Nature was putting us back in our place."

"He sounds like a smart man. I would have liked meeting him. I'm sorry he died."

Peyton tried to go for a casual shrug. "Thanks, but there's no need to be sorry. It's not as if you could have stopped it." She changed the subject before Nixie could reply. "About the water earlier…"

Nixie picked up the stick again and poked the fire. "What about it?"

"You didn't see the dog carcass before you stopped Static." It wasn't a question. She turned to look at her, focusing entirely on her and leaning close. "How did you know?" She should have confronted her when they were in the tent. It would have been easier to detain her if she tried to leave, which is exactly what happened.

Peyton moved quickly, jumping to her feet and grabbing Nixie's upper arm. It was a good thing she was so small. Almost her entire hand fit around her biceps.

Nixie stopped in her tracks and the two of them stood, frozen. "Let me go."

"Where are you going to go? Just answer the question, Nixie. What's going on? Something is on your mind or you would have blown off the question."

"I said, let me go."

"I hate to point it out, but you're outnumbered here. I just have to raise my voice and Jasper will come out. So are you going to sit down and talk about this?" She didn't want to bully her but she didn't have a choice. She needed to know what was going on, and this was the only way she could think of that might work. Such a tactic might have made her feel good a month ago, but now it didn't.

Nixie's muscles were locked with tension, but after a few moments, they relaxed. The fight left her body and she sighed audibly. Peyton loosened her grip just enough to let Nixie turn, but not enough that she would be able to flee if she felt the need to.

"You wouldn't believe me if I told you. Can't you just let it go?"

"No, I can't. I need to know what we're dealing with here. For the safety of my people."

Nixie's laugh was a sharp, harsh sound that grated on Peyton's nerves. "Trust me, I'm harmless. Probably more harmless than Static."

"I don't know, sometimes the smallest people are the fiercest fighters."

The laugh changed, and Peyton didn't want to spend time analyzing why that made her feel better.

Nixie sat on the ground next to her and Peyton released her arm, joining her. She sat close, but not so close as to make her feel like she was being crowded, even though the desire to wrap an arm around her shoulder nearly overwhelmed her, and not just to keep her from fleeing. She clenched her hands and thrust them into her lap to keep them in place. "Try me."

Nixie took a deep breath and sighed again, looking down at the ground. Her fingertips brushed against some dirt and started tracing seemingly random patterns. Bits of grass and twigs were rearranged. Peyton wondered if she'd actually say anything.

"I can find water." Her shoulders drooped as she said it, and her head bowed so low she almost touched it against her knees. "With my body."

That one word flooded back to Peyton. *Power.* So, she had been right, however far-fetched it seemed. Maybe her instincts weren't so bad after all. "Water witch," Peyton replied smoothly. When Nixie jerked her head back to look at her, Peyton nodded. "I thought the Travelers had been making up stories. I guess not. Maybe they're right about everything. Maybe Static's rebuilt city exists, too. It's certainly a lot more believable than this." She picked up the stick Nixie had abandoned and poked the fire. The logs shifted, sending a burst of sparks skyward, and Nixie started. "They didn't mention you could tell the difference between clean and tainted water, though."

"Yes."

"How?"

She shrugged. "I don't know how it works scientifically. I just know the water feels…wrong. I can smell it."

"How can you smell it? I smelled the water. I mean, yeah, it was a little stagnant, but still."

"It's hard to describe. It just smells *wrong* to me. And I get a kind of sense about it. Sometimes the scent is weak. Other times it's overpowering. It makes me feel sick in a way. Like I'm poisoned."

Peyton tried to wrap her mind around this news. *How is any of this possible?* It just seemed so strange. Dad's voice came back again, urging Peyton to trust Nixie. "How sensitive are your abilities?"

"It depends on the volume of water. It's easier when it's a large body, but to determine if the water is pure or not, I need to be closer. Almost on top of it. I can sense rainstorms in the distance. If I concentrate hard enough and focus my body, I can find minute amounts, but it's exhausting. It throws me off and I'm usually stumbling around after. I need to rest frequently."

Minute amounts.

Stumbling around.

Rest.

Peyton jolted upright and turned to Nixie. She'd kept her reason for being at the Mill a secret for so long.

Nixie blinked at her, eyes wide. "What?"

"You were at the Mill to steal filtration equipment."

Nixie winced and hunched her shoulders. It was answer enough. "No sense denying it I guess," she answered weakly. "Yeah, we took it. But you have to understand, we were desperate. And if it took you this long to figure it out, without even noticing it was gone, was it something you really needed?" She held her hands out, palms up, as if offering peace.

And surprisingly, Peyton wasn't angry. "But if you can find water, why?"

"Most of the water sources I've found need to be filtered. Not everything is taken out in boiling the water. It's difficult. We need a lot of water, and with boiling, we can only do so much at a time. Water sources are getting harder to find. Without any rain, all the levels are low. Dramatically lower than a few years ago, when it wasn't nearly this bad. We had sources, and it was okay. We camped near a stream that ran strong enough. But it dried out, and we had to move. You know how bad it is," she implored. "You've seen your crops burning. You heard Mrs. Burgoine and Cooper talking. At least you have food in storage. We never get enough. And if your foraging trips are turning up empty, imagine how it is for us when that's all we rely on."

Peyton turned her words over, sensing the desperation in her voice as she rushed her words at the end. "Did you get what you needed?"

Nixie nodded. "Yes. I'm sorry, I really am."

"I guess you did what you had to do."

"You're not angry?"

Peyton thought about it. Was she angry? Should she be? Probably. Willow would be upset. Jasper, too. Ryan would be downright furious. But Graham and Old Joe? They'd probably understand. Dad would have understood. She turned her gaze to Nixie. "I probably should be, but no, I'm not angry."

"That is the biggest relief." Nixie's lips curled up into the widest smile Peyton had seen from her since they'd met, and damn if she didn't look even more beautiful with the glow from the fire brightening her face.

CHAPTER NINETEEN

A thousand pounds of pressure lifted off Nixie's shoulders when Peyton said that. She hadn't realized she'd even been holding it until that moment. It really *was* the biggest relief to know the guard wasn't angry with her, at least not for that. Inexplicably, she wanted Peyton to like her. The guilt of knowing how her father had died and who had been responsible for his death still sat squarely on her shoulders, but she fought to push it away. Some things were better left unsaid, and even if she yearned to unburden herself, it was too late. She had waited too long.

They talked after that for some time, with the moon passing over them. Nixie's eyelids started to droop and Peyton caught it after the third time. "Get some sleep. If we break camp tomorrow, we'll be leaving early."

"Don't you need someone to keep you awake?"

Peyton chuckled. "No, it's fine. I've done this before. Besides, I'll wake Jasper in a few hours and he'll take my place."

Nixie mumbled a vague agreement before crawling into the tent. The quarters were close and the ground was hard even with the sleeping mats put down. She pulled the blanket over her as a light cover and had barely put her head down before she fell asleep. Her dreams were filled with chaos. People screaming, gunshots fired. The stench of copper filled the air, flooding her senses and blocking out the crisp water, even as she stood in it. The air split above her and a bolt of lightning cracked, striking a tree nearby. Louder screams. Burning hair and flesh. Cries of pain. Someone laughing. A child crying. Nixie bolted upright, drawing in a deep breath, as alert as if she had been awake for hours rather than seconds. Beside her, Peyton lay motionless.

For a guard, she doesn't wake easily. The thought filled her with wonder and a brief moment of concern, but Peyton had to be tired. Besides, Jasper was watching out for them. She leaned forward and pushed the flap of the tent aside and saw him sitting in front of the gently flickering flames, his back to her, as he surveyed the landscape.

What a lonely job, to sit there all night.

She lay back down, aware of Peyton by her side. Though the night was warm, she didn't mind the heat from Peyton's body. It was different from the day's humidity. Instead of being oppressive and uncomfortable, it made her feel safe and relaxed, as though she didn't have to worry about anything at that moment.

Peyton rolled over in her sleep and flung out an arm. Nixie started when it landed on her waist. The arm reflexively tightened, and Nixie held her breath, waiting for Peyton to wake up and realize what she'd done. Instead, she kept sleeping, her breathing deep and even.

Should I move? But if I move, I could wake her up.

Don't be an idiot, she didn't wake up after your nightmare. She isn't going to wake up if you move her arm.

Still, it feels kind of nice...

And it did feel nice. She wanted the contact. So she quelled the dueling voices in her mind and closed her eyes, allowing herself to relax into the touch. Soon she matched Peyton's breathing, and the gentle sound lulled her to sleep.

The next morning, Nixie woke to the solid press of a warm body against hers. She sighed and, despite the warmth of the early morning sun heating up the inside of the tent, curled up tighter, resting her head on the firm shoulder.

Her eyes snapped open.

Firm shoulder?

Oh, shit.

Her eyes were only a few inches away from Peyton's exposed neck. She blinked away the sleep, trying to slowly shift away from her so as not to wake her and be caught in such a compromising position.

"Good morning," Peyton said, her tone light. She chuckled, and Nixie's face burned hotter than boiling water. "You seemed comfortable, so I didn't want to wake you."

"I am so sorry," she mumbled before pulling away. She quickly rolled onto her side to hide the color, but Peyton laughed again.

"It's fine. You needed the sleep after yesterday. We're going to have another long day today."

She rose from her sleeping mat and crawled to the door. Once outside and out of sight, Nixie fell onto her back with a groan and covered her face with her hands.

Peyton heard the groan and smiled to herself. True, it had been a surprise to wake up to Nixie curled up in her arms, pressed tightly against her, but it had been far from unpleasant. Quite the opposite, in fact. Nixie looked peaceful when she slept, and she sometimes mumbled strange things. Oddly enough, Peyton liked it.

Despite neither of them having bathed since the night before they started their journey, after the long, grueling hike in the hot sun, Nixie smelled clean, like crisp, cool water. She wondered if it was because of her abilities. Did she always exude that clean scent? Was it only when she slept? Or when she was calm? Peyton wanted to find out.

Jasper stirred the fire, adding another branch to it. He glanced at her before grunting something like, "Good morning."

"How was the watch?"

"Boring as usual. I didn't expect there to be any problems. Not even an animal."

"A pity for you. I'll take care of getting breakfast started. Go rest for a while. Check on Static."

"What time do you want to head out?"

Peyton glanced up at the sky. The sun had just peeked above the horizon and cast a pleasant glow over the land. In the distance, the light bounced off the still intact windows of skyscrapers. The heat had dissipated and made the morning air feel almost cool against her skin.

"Before the sun is up too far. We'll be in the shadows mostly once we get into the city, but I'd rather not deal with too much heat if we can avoid it. Let him sleep as long as he needs, though. We can also have breakfast ready for him and head out right after."

"Okay."

"If Cooper is awake, send him out. I'll have him scout the area for more food. Might as well load up before we head into the city—might be there awhile."

Jasper nodded and turned back to his tent. As soon as he disappeared and the flap shut behind him, Nixie emerged from their shared tent. She tried to smooth her hair back, but some strands stuck out in a fuzzy halo around her head.

"Is there anything I can do to help?" she asked as she approached the fire.

Peyton handed her the empty pot. "We could use some more water"—she offered her a smile—"for breakfast. And then we need to filter as much as we can carry."

Nixie nodded and took the pot.

"Can you tell whether or not there's any water in the city?"

She hesitated. "Once we pass the river, I'll be able to focus on it. Right now there's too much water in between and I can't separate them."

"What do you think the chances are for actually finding water in the city?"

Nixie frowned, deep in thought. "I don't remember seeing any the last time we went in. I don't know it well. Although if it rained hard enough—"

Peyton interrupted with a snort.

Nixie glared. "If the rain was hard enough, then there might be something left. How safe it will be? Probably not very. I wouldn't even filter it."

"What would you do?"

"You're asking for my advice?"

Peyton nodded. Yes, she was. When it came to water, Peyton would defer to her, just as she would defer to Cooper in terms of foraging or Static regarding radios.

"Set up camp on the other side of the river. Not next to it, but close enough that we could get potable water easily. More firewood available, too. There won't be any in the city, and we need it to boil the water at the very least."

Peyton hadn't thought of that. "So we should move camp to the other side and set up before we search?"

"It would make it easier to come back to a camp already set up," Nixie said with a shrug. "Plus we'll be able to move faster without all the gear on our backs."

"What about Scavengers?"

"My people don't travel into the city. I can't be sure of others, but I don't see why any group would. There aren't enough resources left to sustain a group for any period of time."

Peyton agreed, absorbing the sound advice. It would surprise the others, but she would follow it and show Nixie that she trusted her. After all, last night Nixie had trusted Peyton enough to be honest and give her details about her abilities. Most others would hide that for as long as possible. And it wasn't exactly as if Peyton had pushed her into giving up her secret. Funny how things could change in a month. "Thank you." She smiled.

Nixie ducked her head and turned toward the river. "I'll just go get the water."

Peyton thanking her? *Is it because of what I told her last night? But why would she listen to me? I have no experience.* Nixie wanted to push the thought from her mind, but it stuck like a fly on honey. Peyton had been genuinely thankful. It stirred warm feelings in her chest, and she wanted more of it, but it stirred other things, too. Guilt about her deception. Burden over her terrible secret. Fear of getting closer, in case that secret came to light and destroyed everything they'd begun to build between them...

Despite her confidence when she'd been talking to Peyton, the doubt began to plague her, so she shook that away as well, focusing on her chore. If Peyton didn't think her ideas were good, she would ignore her advice. She knew what she was doing, even if she was new to leading people.

Once Nixie had collected the water, trying to skim off the muck before bringing it back into the camp, she set it on the fire to boil. Another empty pot sat close by and she repeated the motions without another word to Peyton. When she returned from her second trip, Cooper took the water from her and ran it through the filter. It amazed her to see cloudy liquid filled with tiny floating bits of algae and bacteria run through the filtration system and come out clear. To her, more than her own abilities, *that* was magic.

"It's a series of tubes and filters," Cooper was saying. She looked up at him and he gestured to the equipment, and then launched into an explanation as if he had been reading her mind.

"What if it breaks? How do you know?"

"The water doesn't come out as clear. We check it after every trip to make sure no parts are wearing down. Wouldn't be good if someone took it out and needed it, only to find it not working properly."

"What happens if they do break?"

"We fix them."

Not only did they have this life-giving equipment, but they could fix whatever broke. Whenever her people broke something, it had to be discarded. No one knew—or remembered—how to fix it. Even if they did, it wasn't like they had a surplus of materials to use.

Static finally emerged from the tent. Jasper, yawning and stretching, followed close behind. Peyton handed both Jasper and Static a mug of some herbal tea. They accepted it with murmured thanks and sat, side by side.

"How are you feeling?" Peyton asked Static as he sipped at the brew.

His face still burned red, but it did not look as desperate as the day before. His shoulders slumped as he sat, but he was able to move. "Tired, but I can do it."

"I didn't ask if you could do it. I asked how you felt. Be straight with me, Static."

"Yes, Mom," he said with a roll of his eyes.

Jasper snickered into his mug.

"I'm tired and a little sore. My shoulders are stiff, like they're tense, but I don't have a headache and I don't feel nauseous."

"That's good," Cooper replied. "The medicine and salve worked. Dr. Easton will be happy to get this report."

"So what are the plans for today?" Jasper asked. He turned and shook the mug to remove the final drops and dry it.

"We're going to move camp to the other side of the river and set up there."

The boys looked at her, mouths twisted in frowns of confusion.

"Set up over there? Why?" Cooper asked.

"We need to be looking *in* the city, not on the edges," Static argued.

"Shouldn't we set up at night where we are?" Jasper added. "If we wander too far away, we'll get stranded without our gear."

"We won't get stranded. We'll keep an eye on the sun and where we are." Peyton glanced at Nixie before addressing the boys. "We don't know if we're going to find water in the city. We need to stay where we have an abundant source. I'm not going to risk having what happened to Static happen again to someone else."

"She's right," Cooper said after a moment. "It would be better. We can only carry a finite amount of water. We'll just have to map out the roads we take. It'll make for slower going, but we'll be able to find our way back easier."

"Should we split up and search?" came Static's question. "We can cover more ground that way."

"Absolutely not." Peyton's hair flew out as she shook her head vehemently, as if the very idea offended her. "We don't have enough resources to divide up. What if someone gets hurt? Nixie can't carry someone back. And I'm not saying we will, but what if we run into a wild animal or Scavengers?"

Cooper and Jasper darted their glances away from Nixie and quickly busied themselves, and when she tried to catch Static's attention, he scratched his head and kicked at the dirt. Despite getting to know each other on this trip, despite all her help, why did they still turn away from her whenever they heard the word Scavenger?

CHAPTER TWENTY

Though the bridge had begun to decay from the lack of use and repair over the last twenty years, it was stable enough for the group to cross. They trekked down to the riverbank and found a good flat spot away from the river's edge, where trees shaded the area. It almost mirrored the place they had slept the night before. It took less time for the group to set up camp, and Peyton surveyed the landscape. She didn't see any signs of recent human activity, so they wouldn't have a problem with leaving their gear behind.

Cooper found some fallen branches and carried them to the site. They had full canteens of water and Jasper slathered Static's face in the salve once again.

"Which direction should we take?" Jasper asked as he put the container back in his bag. "The city is huge." He turned to Nixie. "Are you sure you don't remember where you were?"

Peyton hoped she remembered something, because, up close, the abandoned city looked even more intimidating than she had imagined. Inside would be a labyrinth of streets, little to no access to water, and no food. Who knew what conditions the streets would be in? And what if someone was injured? They were hours—if not days—from help.

Nixie turned toward the city, her face scrunching as she concentrated. "We traveled on the highway, looking for promising places. We took one of the exits but I don't remember which one. I know it wasn't immediately beyond the river."

"Would you remember what it looked like if we stuck to the highway?"

Again the scrunch as she concentrated; Peyton wanted to smooth the wrinkles away. Her eyes took on a distant look, as if she were trying to see the past. "I can't make promises, but maybe seeing it will trigger my memory."

They all turned to Peyton then and she nodded, decision made. "Then we stick to the highway. It's the best option we have right now. We should be able to see more, too. Take the gear you need, but leave the rest here."

Everyone nodded and gathered their things. Peyton pulled Nixie aside, turning away from the group so no one could eavesdrop. "Any idea on the water situation in the city yet?"

"Not a drop."

Peyton swore softly and Nixie murmured her agreement. "As long as we're out of the city before the sun hits the horizon, we'll be okay."

"We're ready to go," Jasper announced from somewhere close behind. Peyton hoped he hadn't overheard anything.

"Good, then let's get a move on."

Abandoned vehicles clogged some areas of the highway, as if they had all been dropped there at once. Peyton didn't understand how it could happen, but so many things During Collapse confused everyone, especially those who had never experienced it. After was all she knew. Before was a foreign concept she just couldn't grasp.

Seeing the heaps of metal, now rusted from being exposed to the elements but still mostly intact, made her feel as if she were in an alien world. She'd never seen a vehicle that ran. Why had the people Before not pushed for alternative sources for fuel?

"I wish I could drive one of these," Jasper said, his voice hushed as he looked across the makeshift graveyard spread out before them. He touched one of the cars, the red paint still visible in some places.

"We'll get the world back someday," Static said, no longer bouncing with each step. Peyton had noticed his decline in energy as they walked. At first she didn't know if he was hurting from the burn or needed to rest, but she came to realize he was mourning the world he'd lost before he'd ever had a chance to live in it.

"I wouldn't even know where to start," Cooper said, shaking his head. "Everything's a mess."

"Start small. Build up. One piece at a time." They all turned to Static as he said it. Peyton had never seen him so solemn before. So calm. The effect was eerie and left her with chills running down her spine. *Maybe he* will *reconnect us.* It was the first time since they'd started their crazy mission that she thought maybe, just maybe, it was possible. If a girl could sense water with her body, then a boy could rebuild a radio and make it work, right?

"We need to keep moving. Stop gawking at the cars and walk," she said after a few more solemn moments of silence. Nixie smiled up at her as she walked by, then fell into step behind her. At each exit they approached, they would stop to let Nixie get her bearings. Sometimes she would say no immediately and they would keep walking. Other times they would pause and she would close her eyes, tilting her head first one way and then the other. Once she started down the exit ramp, convinced she had the right one, only to get to the end and turn them back around.

"I'm sorry," she whispered to Peyton.

"Nothing to be sorry for," she replied, content with resting a hand on Nixie's shoulder when she really wanted to pull her in for a hug. "Without you we'd be even more lost on the city streets right now. Probably facing a Minotaur or something," she added teasingly.

"What's a Minotaur?"

"Greek mythology?"

Nixie just stared blankly and Peyton told her to forget about it. It was getting easier with each passing moment to forget about their differences. In the past twenty-four hours, Nixie had managed to blend into the group. There had been that odd moment last night after Peyton mentioned Scavengers, but today that weird tension was absent. Cooper no longer looked at her strangely. Sometimes when she said something, he laughed or added his own comments. Nixie took to Static like a mother hen, and he allowed it. Jasper teased her good-naturedly like he did with Willow. When Graham asked what Peyton would do with Nixie, she had only considered making her a part of their group to appease him. Now the idea didn't seem as far-fetched anymore. Indeed, it sounded downright alluring.

CHAPTER TWENTY-ONE

This is it. This is definitely it," Nixie announced. She stared at the weathered green sign announcing exit forty-two. She looked around, and fragments of images flickered through her mind: Ranger suggesting they get off the old highway and find shelter for the night. One of his men arguing that it was easier to just keep moving on until they reached the river. Ranger wanting to check out the area and scout for supplies. A scuffle.

Nixie looked down at the pavement, expecting to see the blood from the other man's head still staining the surface, but nothing remained. It would have been washed away by one of the infrequent rainstorms. It had seemed like so much blood then, but now Nixie knew what it looked like when a man was killed. That had been just a scratch. "Head wounds bleed a lot," Ranger had told her afterward, when she'd screamed at them to quit it. She wondered how they were faring without her now that they had the water filter. Why hadn't he tried to come back for her? Or had he, and Peyton hid it from her?

"Are you sure?" Peyton asked, yanking her back to the present from her reverie.

"Positive." Nixie pushed the sudden flare of doubt from her mind and gestured down the ramp. "It's coming back to me now. I remember we stopped here. There was an argument." She recalled the rest of her vision to them, leaving out their names, and then started down the ramp, sure that they would follow her.

They did.

Peyton pulled up next to her, keeping pace and constantly scanning the area. She was good at that, and Nixie admired how vigilant she was. She felt perfectly safe knowing Peyton was keeping tabs on their surroundings. Sometimes she would get lost in her own thoughts and Ranger would yell at her to snap out of it. He didn't mean it to be nasty. Not usually. He wanted to protect her and make sure she could defend herself, which was hard to do when lost in a daydream—like she was right now. Peyton looked at her expectantly and she looked at the ground to hide the fact that her cheeks were burning. "Sorry, what was that?"

The guard chuckled. "I asked which way to go now. We're at the end of the ramp."

Oh.

So they were.

Nixie surveyed the area. Not much had changed that she could tell. "Straight ahead. We'll run into a field. I think."

"You think?" Jasper muttered from behind. She felt Peyton turn and could only imagine the look she shot him. He stopped talking.

"Yes, I think. I know there's a field somewhere. I'm sorry, but I'm doing my best."

A warm, comforting hand rested on her shoulder and Peyton leaned closer. "Just ignore him." To the rest of the group she said, "We'll get there. Without Nixie we wouldn't have even crossed the river."

The road of houses had long since been abandoned. Many of them had burned in a fire, and others had been vandalized. Messages were scrawled over the buildings, some common graffiti, others religious messages of repentance and salvation. Nixie hardly glanced at them as they moved along, though she did hear Static murmur something inaudible behind her to one of the boys. A large, empty field stood before them at the end of the road and Nixie smiled in triumph. At this rate, they'd be there in no time.

"Nice sized plot of land," Cooper noted. "It would be a perfect place to grow crops if it were closer to the river."

"That's probably why no one settled here," Jasper added. "It's too far out of the way. A shame, too. It would be nice to start resettling the cities."

Static chimed in with, "If we get the radio parts, it'll be easier to do that. We can expand and have more room to make advances again."

Nixie glanced up at the clear blue sky. The sun burned down on them still, but it wasn't as hot as the day before. "Let's get moving," she said. "It shouldn't be too much farther ahead." With Nixie's lead, they turned right down the street and continued to walk. There were fewer vehicles this way, and of those that remained, many were burned out husks.

"The riots," Static said. "I remember Old Joe telling us about them."

It wasn't just the vehicles. Windows on houses and storefronts were smashed. Many of the buildings were brick, and scorch marks scarred the surfaces. Static poked his head into one of the gaping holes and looked around.

"This one has been looted."

Inside were empty shelving units. One or two stood upright, but the majority had been tipped over and lay on the floor or leaned up against others. Not a single item had been left behind, but even if it had, chances were it would be useless by now. Nixie turned and stared down the road, a frown pulling at her lips. Something didn't feel right. This place didn't feel familiar. She wracked her brain, trying to recall the direction they took after the field, and she thought it was to the right.

Maybe we just need to go a little farther. So much of the city looks like this. It's not like out in Vernon.

"Let's keep moving. There's nothing here for us," Peyton urged, her eyes constantly scanning the area. Jasper engaged in much the same behavior, scanning in the opposite direction. Nixie could tell just by watching them that they had been trained well together. Whenever one turned, the other watched their back. A perfect pair. A surge of jealousy rose in Nixie that she didn't understand. What reason did she have to be jealous? They had grown up together. They were friends; they worked together. She scowled, directing it at herself, and stalked off.

"Hey! Wait up!" Cooper called.

The pounding feet grew closer and Peyton materialized at her side. "Don't just wander off without us."

"Not like I went far," she muttered.

"What's up?"

Nixie shook her head. She didn't want to answer that question. Hell, she didn't think she could even if she wanted to. "We just need to keep moving," she said in response.

Peyton didn't believe the tepid answer, but she followed Nixie as she kept walking. With Jasper behind her scanning the shops as they passed in case she missed something in the first sweep, she knew they were completely safe. In fact, it was hard not to let herself be lulled into a false sense of security. Nothing moved. Precious few sounds even reached her ears. Sometimes a bird would wheel in the sky above them and call out to its companions, and a faint response could be heard from the distance. Not even a single animal seemed to be left in the city. Peyton had read that animals had remained in the cities after people had left, but there were none here, probably due to the lack of food. But every so often, where the pavement had been cracked, a sapling pushed out, spreading its branches toward the sky. Trees that lined the sidewalks had grown larger, and their roots pushed the ground up, breaking the concrete and making passage difficult at times. Dad said Mother Nature was reclaiming what had been taken from her. Someday the animals would be back, and maybe humans, too.

The group continued walking, but with each new side street they passed, Nixie grew more agitated. Peyton could tell by the way her shoulders tensed and how she kept glancing back at them. She wanted to ask what the problem was but refrained, after the way she'd been shrugged off earlier.

"Down here," Nixie said sharply, picking up the pace as she took a side street. They didn't question as they followed her down one street after another. Soon they twisted and turned, taking every other street in a new direction. Peyton tried to keep track of the turns in her head, but soon she'd forgotten. It was a good thing Cooper had that map, otherwise they'd be screwed.

Nixie's usual calm demeanor faded as she glanced around at the passing buildings. Her eyes were wide, her lips tightened in a grimace. She darted down a narrow side street and they followed, only to stop abruptly at the dead end in front of them.

The wall from a building had partially collapsed, and the rubble blocked their progress. True, they could climb over and resume their mission, but judging by the look on Nixie's face, things were not good.

"Let's stop here and take a break," Peyton ordered, forcing the words past her lips as Cooper pulled Jasper aside and mumbled something in his ear.

Three of her companions nodded and dropped to the ground, rummaging through their packs for food, but ahead of her Nixie stood statue still, staring at the blockade.

Peyton grasped Nixie's arm and pulled her out of hearing range of the others. She maneuvered them out of sight of the others. "What's going on?" she asked, consciously keeping her voice low and her tone light. The last thing she needed was to freak Nixie out and cause her to bolt.

"It's just a little more," Nixie replied, her voice quiet. Weak. Not like her at all.

"We're lost, aren't we?" When Nixie burst into tears, she took a step back. She wasn't expecting that reaction.

"I'm so sorry. I thought I knew where we were going, and I was so sure it was down this way, but I think at the field we were supposed to go left or keep going straight or something, but I don't remember which and instead I turned us right and that was the wrong thing to do. What if we can't get back in time before nightfall and we're trapped in the city or we—"

"Stop," she ordered, grabbing Nixie by the shoulders and pulling her close to shake her a little.

"We could be completely turned around and run out of water and then what do we do?"

"It's not going to happen. Cooper has a map and you can sense the river, right? Calm down. We're *fine*."

"We're not. This is a mistake, this is such a mistake! How could I have thought I could lead us to the place?"

Peyton sighed. Evidently she wasn't going to listen to reason. She shook the slender young woman again, shifting her hands from her arms to her face and locking her in place.

"I mean, Faulkner never even trusted me to leave the camp without a guard"—Nixie continued, undeterred—"let alone act on my own. I can't believe I—"

"Stop," Peyton repeated, but this time instead of letting her ramble on, she pulled her close and did the only thing she could to shut her up: she pressed her lips to Nixie's mouth.

It worked.

Nixie gasped, her mouth pulling into a firm line before going slack under Peyton's. Her whole body went limp and Peyton found herself holding the Scavenger up. Her lips were deceptively soft and smooth and tasted sweet. Nixie tensed up at first, but then relaxed in her arms. Peyton wanted to stay there all day. After a few breathless moments, Peyton released her enough to look into her eyes. They were wide, but the fright had faded to curiosity. "Are you done?"

Nixie nodded.

"Good." She released her gradually, making sure she would be able to stand on her feet before taking a step back. She cleared her throat. "Cooper has a map. We're not lost. We can reference it and figure out where we are and then backtrack to the field."

"I'm sorry I got us lost," Nixie stuttered. Her face colored a shade of purple Peyton hadn't thought possible on a human, and she worried she would pass out.

"It happens." Peyton tried to ignore it. She needed to focus on the task at hand, not what had just happened, and definitely not how it made her feel. What the hell had she been thinking, kissing her like that? She had enough problems without adding to the list.

"But what if the sun sets?" Nixie sounded breathless. "I suggested we make the camp before we set out."

"And I listened. It will be on me, not you."

Nixie wasn't having it, apparently, because she continued to argue, her voice rising in pitch. "How will they trust me after this?"

Peyton shrugged. "We're here. We'll keep looking. Things go wrong sometimes. We'll just pick ourselves back up and keep moving." *It's what Dad would have done. Maybe I'm more like him than I thought.* The idea warmed her, and she smiled. "Now, eat something and rest up. Cooper and I will figure out where we are and we'll go from there."

Nixie nodded and sank to the ground behind the rubble. She looked like she wanted to be alone for a while, and Peyton could respect that. After all, she had preferred to pass her time that way, too. Until recently, at least.

Pressing her fingers against her lips, Peyton rounded the corner of the rubble to find Cooper and Jasper looking up at her expectantly from their seats on the ground. She joined them, digging into her pack and pulling out the dried meat and berries. She studiously avoided looking them in the eyes, worried they'd see what she'd just done and realize it had affected her more than she wanted to admit. She could still feel Nixie's warmth against her lips and the gentle tingles it sent through her body.

"We need your map," she said to Cooper after she'd kept them waiting long enough to pop one of the berries into her mouth. With considerable effort, she forced thoughts of Nixie from her mind. She'd deal with the kiss later.

He grumbled. "I figured as much." The map came out of his pocket and he unfolded it and then set it on the ground between them. "I've been trying to keep the turns she's taken us on straight, but I'm a little mixed up."

"Me, too," Jasper chimed in. "Wish she'd have just told us before that we'd taken a wrong turn," he grumbled, "rather than leading us on a wild goose chase."

"She's nervous. Doesn't want to let us down." Peyton defended her, but there didn't seem to be a need. They just shrugged it off and put their heads together to look at the map.

"This is the field we were at before," Cooper said, gently poking at the map with his index finger. Let's see where we ended up."

They tried to trace their first route but ended up searching over the entire map before finding the street they were off. Jasper let out a low whistle. "Damn. We're pretty far out. But at least we know where we are, right? We can make a straight line back to the park and go from there again."

"What are the chances of us making it back before dark?"

"To the river?" Peyton nodded. "Not a chance," Jasper said, peering up at the sky. The color was still bright blue and clear, but the light had faded just enough to let them know it was late afternoon. "But we should be able to make it back to the field by then."

"What do you suggest? Should we camp at the field and try to correct our course in the morning, or push to get to the river in the dark?"

Cooper and Jasper stared at her silently for a moment before Jasper chimed in with, "You're asking for our advice?"

Peyton shrugged, recalling the words her father had said to her. *A good leader doesn't just lead. They ask for help when they need it and work with their group.* Okay, so maybe she wasn't explicitly asking for help, but it was kind of the same thing, right? She'd asked Nixie for her help earlier, without dire consequences. She needed to let more people in, and she would. Starting today. "I'd like to know what everyone wants. If you think it best to make it to the camp for the night, even if it means traveling in the dark, then we do it."

Cooper nodded and glanced over her shoulder to where Static rested. "Traveling at night in this unfamiliar area wouldn't be the wisest choice. Even with the light of the moon, it would be too dark to see clearly, and we could end up getting hurt."

Jasper nodded. "True, and it would be just as easy to camp at the field. But a majority of our supplies are at the riverbank. Do we want to spend a night without them? In the end, it's your call, Peyton."

Peyton agreed. Didn't she know it? "We camp at the field, then. Map out our route. We leave in ten minutes."

"Ten?" Jasper asked. "We could leave in five."

"I know, but I want Static to rest as much now as possible." She glanced back at him. His head had drooped and his chin was propped on his chest. The four of them might be able to make it back to the river uninjured, but frankly, she didn't think Static would.

And he couldn't afford an injury on top of his burn, dehydration, and exhaustion.

CHAPTER TWENTY-TWO

It wasn't much of a camp, but it would have to do. As things stood, it wasn't the best Nixie had spent a night in, but it also wasn't the worst. Besides, she couldn't complain. It was her fault, after all. If she had just admitted that they were lost when she'd first realized it, they could have turned around and made it back to the field well before nightfall. But no. She had to keep going, pushing herself further, just in case she was mistaken.

What an idiot.

She sat alone off to the side. The others weren't angry, but she felt terrible about the situation, especially because of Static. He looked so miserable with the burn covering his face. Jasper dipped his fingers in the salve, glancing into the jar and at what covered his fingertips. With a sigh, he gently eased it on Static's face.

"The burn will fade into a nice tan," Jasper teased. "Maybe you'll finally get yourself a girl and not scare them off looking like a ghost."

Static snorted loudly but didn't respond.

Cooper tended to the small fire he had built. Like the camp, it wasn't much, but it would heat their food and keep any animals away from their site.

Nixie glanced at Peyton, who sat off to the side. When Peyton had kissed her back in that alley, all thoughts had completely fled her mind. It had felt nice, once she'd relaxed into it. She'd never been kissed before; she had to smile at that. Her first kiss had come from someone she used to hate. It might have been used as a way to shut her up, but she'd felt something deeper in that kiss. Something different. Peyton could have pulled away long before she did—she could have, too—but they'd both wanted to prolong the contact. She glanced at where Peyton was looking at the map and then back down at the scribbles she'd scratched in the dirt. She'd wanted a connection with someone for so long and it was just her luck the person was a Settler. A beautiful Settler, with long blond hair, who was fiercely protective of her friends.

The ground was hard beneath her, but she lay down anyway, using the pack to cushion her head. She'd eaten a small portion of her food to regain her strength and sipped at her water enough to keep her hydrated. She would have liked more, but her idiocy had ruined that. *Stop. Stop blaming yourself. Peyton doesn't, and neither do the others.* Nixie sighed and turned her back to the fire, closing her eyes. Even when she tried to block it out, she could still feel the press of those lips against hers. They'd been dry, and just a little cracked. Nixie worried Peyton was dehydrated, but she couldn't exactly produce water to solve that problem.

That's good. Focus on Peyton's physical well-being rather than how the kiss felt.

As if she could actually do that...

Peyton tasted like blackberries. Had she been eating some as they walked? Nixie couldn't remember. She'd been too busy freaking out over getting them lost. But that sweet taste had been as unexpected as the kiss. She turned her face into the pack to muffle a groan. Who was she fooling? Certainly not herself. If she was honest about everything, she'd admit she was falling for Peyton. And if that didn't just beat everything, she didn't know what did. What would Ranger think if he knew what was going through her mind right now? What about Faulkner? She shuddered to think about that one, so it was best to push it from her mind. Ranger, on the other hand...she didn't mind thinking about him. She missed him. As stubborn as he could be, he'd always been decent to her. He looked out for her on missions, and knowing him, he'd probably laugh at the lunacy of her situation.

Good. Think about Ranger instead of the kiss.

That's distracting enough.

Had it really been nearly a month since her mistake had separated them? It didn't seem that long, now that she thought about it. She could only assume the others made it back okay and that the water filtration system was working. They would have figured out how to run it, right? It didn't seem so difficult once Cooper had shown her the method.

Why hadn't they come back to check on her?

She hadn't heard a single person mention having seen Scavengers in the area. Had her people given her up as a lost cause? Had Ranger figured she'd make it out on her own? Or had Faulkner told them to forget about her and move on? A thought struck her then—what if they had left? What if Faulkner had gotten what he wanted and ordered them to break camp? It would make sense. With her captured, maybe he thought the Settlers would torture her to get information, and Faulkner probably figured she'd break and spill their secrets. Moving everyone was the safe thing to do. Better to lose one than the whole group, right? But what secrets did he have that he would want to keep, aside from her abilities?

And why did the idea of being left behind hurt so damn much?

A blind man could see Nixie had nightmares that night. At first Peyton had been concerned when she chose a spot on the other side of the fire from the boys, alone, but then realized it might be for the best once her thrashing began. Once or twice she let out a short whimper, but that was it. Her limbs, on the other hand, were weapons flailing through the air.

"Should you wake her up?" Jasper whispered as he rose to take her place for the rest of the watch.

"I don't know. Dad always said to let sleeping dogs lie."

"Does that look like sleeping to you?"

"Not really."

"Besides, she's not a dog."

"No," Peyton assented, "but she is fierce enough to bite."

Jasper chuckled. "That little thing? I doubt it. You're getting soft on her."

Peyton looked at him in alarm. Could he see? Did he know how her feelings were changing? *Had* changed?

"Nice way to shut her up, by the way. I've got to try that myself sometime. Hmm…I wonder who it would work best on."

He had seen. Damn. Peyton punched his arm lightly. "You go kissing the boys and you won't get the same reaction I got."

"Not if they like me." He paused. "Because she does, you know. Like you."

"Of course she must like me," Peyton said, getting up to stretch and mask her discomfort with the subject. She didn't want to discuss personal issues with Jasper, even if he was one of her best friends. She didn't do the whole personal thing. Even if she was trying to trust him more on other matters, discussing her bewildering feelings for Nixie was a step too far. "She wouldn't have agreed to this mission if she outright hated me."

"You're not an idiot, Pey. You know what I'm talking about."

She knew, all right. Which is why she waved him off, dismissing him for the night, and paced to the opposite side of the fire from where he sat. She wouldn't sleep near Static and Cooper, but as much as she would have liked the warmth of sleeping next to Nixie, she was going to be sleeping alone tonight. *I just don't want to get hit with flailing limbs*, she reasoned.

Of course.

That made perfect sense.

When she looked across the fire to see Jasper grinning at her, looking like a demon with the fire in his eyes and brightening his teeth, she merely flipped him off with a huff. What the hell did he know, after all?

CHAPTER TWENTY-THREE

Nixie woke before the others. Jasper was on watch but was doing a poor job of it as he sat slumped over with his head nearly in his lap. When he woke up he would have a terrible crick in his neck. Quietly she rose and crept out of their site. She wanted to try to get her bearings. This time she wouldn't make a mistake. She wouldn't lead them down the wrong path again. As the sun rose, casting an orange glow over the land, she stopped and sniffed the air.

Rain.

Again, there was that tantalizing smell, teasing her, just at the edges of her abilities. It was stronger here and almost called to her. She wanted to follow it, follow the scent, and dance with her arms raised up in the rain.

Closing her eyes she opened her senses completely and let it wash over her, bathing her in the cool crispness. She could almost feel the tiny drops dancing down on her skin, hammering a light staccato beat in time with a roll of thunder. She took one step, then another. Turned. Spun. Allowed herself to become part of the distant storm, wanting it to be closer. If only she could pull it closer, pull the clouds to her and part them over her head. She would gladly drown in the drops, allow her mouth to fill with precious, life-giving liquid and take her away.

"Nixie."

The hand on her shoulder shook her and she forced her eyes open abruptly. The voice sounded urgent, as if it had been calling her for some time. When she turned to face Peyton, she saw the others standing behind her, their eyes fixed to the sky.

"What?" she asked, her voice coming out breathless.

"What did you do?" Peyton demanded. She looked above her, also at the sky.

What was the big deal with the sky? It was always blue. What could possibly be so fascinating? She frowned and tried to pull Peyton's hand from her shoulder, but her fingers had locked into a grip that was unbreakable. Her nails started to dig in and Nixie winced. "Peyton, let go. You're hurting me."

"Nixie, what did you do?" she repeated.

"I didn't do anything! What are you talking about? I was just going to…" She finally followed Peyton's gaze. Rather than a clear bright blue sky tinged with the glow from the rising sun, Nixie stared into the face of the darkest storm cloud she'd ever seen. "Oh, shit."

"Where did that come from?" Static asked, cowering behind Cooper.

Peyton looked down at Nixie, her eyes boring into her.

She couldn't move. "What?" she asked in a whisper.

"Did you do this?"

"No. I don't think so. I've never before—" The low rumble of thunder cut her off. She gaped in awe at the clouds and shivered as the wind picked up.

"We need to move," Peyton barked as the rumble died down. "That storm is going to hit and who knows what it will do. Can you get us to the shop?"

Nixie nodded. "Yes, yes definitely."

"Then let's move!"

"But the fire—"

"Is almost out. Kick some dirt over it, Cooper, and let's go. The rain will take care of it."

Cooper nodded at Peyton's order and the rest scurried to gather their few supplies. Nixie moved, too, but at a slower pace, almost as if she were in a trance.

Where *had* the clouds come from? The storm? She breathed in, closing her eyes as she shouldered her pack and was nearly overwhelmed with the scent of the rain. Had she done this? Called the storm down on them? But *how*?

"Move!" Peyton ordered, looking up at the sky. "I don't want to be in the middle of the field when lightning strikes."

That got Nixie's feet moving. She darted forward with the others, out of the field. When they looked back to her for directions, she took the lead. "This way." Nixie stayed straight on the road, pushing them in a flat-out run as the slow roll of thunder chased them. No houses remained standing on this street, but she could see just ahead, and at the intersection, the road turned residential once again. If they could make it to the first house before the lightning struck, they could hug the buildings the rest of the way to the store and avoid being out in the open.

A flash lit the sky, obscuring everything around her. Nixie stopped in her tracks. The thunderclap that followed deafened her. She saw Peyton's mouth move but couldn't hear the words she spoke. Static's face was distorted, his mouth open comically wide. What had she done? Peyton grabbed her arm and pulled her forward. The momentum nearly pulled Nixie off her feet, but she found her bearings and joined in the stampede.

"...much farther," she heard as her hearing returned to normal. Who had spoken, she couldn't tell, but it didn't matter. The only thing that mattered was getting off the streets.

The street sign, faded with age and half hanging, read *Flatbush Ave*, and she yelled in excitement, "Yes! This is the road! Keep going!" Just like on the other street, some of the houses had been damaged from vandalism or fire, maybe both, but a few stood. She ran toward the first one with the others close on her heels.

The windows had long since been smashed in and she crawled into the lowest one, moving out of the way and helping Static through. He gasped for air as he collapsed against a wall.

"I'm not made for this shit. Please let me go back," he begged.

Peyton crawled in last and looked ready to slap him, but she turned to face the street instead just as another bolt of lightning split the air.

"Well, that was rather unexpected," Cooper said once he'd regained his own breath. "Now what the hell do we do?"

"Who knows how long it will last. We can't just stay here until the storm passes. Can we?" Static asked. He'd slumped down and rested against the floor.

"The good news is you won't get burned anymore," Jasper said. Peyton shot him a glare and Jasper shrugged, holding his hands out in apology.

"No, we won't stay here. We'll just time it and move between the houses."

Nixie cleared her throat and they all turned to look at her. "Up ahead, the houses end. There are parking lots for one block. After that, we turn, and there's more open space."

They groaned.

"Are there any places we can take shelter?" Peyton asked.

"There are a few storefronts along the way. We could always try to run and make it to the next one."

"We have just one huge problem with this whole thing," Cooper said. Everyone turned to look at him. "We get hit by one bolt, and we're all dead."

"Well, we won't really know what hit us, will we?"

Everyone groaned. "Jasper, really?" Peyton said. Her hands twitched and Nixie wondered if she would strangle him then and there, or wait until no one was watching. "Since we didn't exactly get the time to eat, let's do that. We'll go from there. Take ten, rest up, and we'll reassess the situation then." Peyton said this to everyone, but she stared directly at Nixie as she did. They'd be having a discussion in the near future, and Nixie couldn't begin to guess how the guard would react.

❖

When she had woken up to a cool wind blowing and Nixie… dancing…across the field, Peyton knew something was incredibly wrong. The clouds had appeared as if by magic, and the young water witch still spun as if in a trance. Nixie might not have been aware of what she was doing, but Peyton could feel whatever it was she'd done. It echoed in her bones, making her body ache as the clouds crashed together. Now, sitting in the remnants of someone's home, she chewed her food thoughtfully.

Well, this is a new situation. What exactly are the protocols for this one, Dad?

Of course he wouldn't respond. He couldn't, and not just because he was dead. As far as she knew, nothing like this had ever happened before. Sure, it was just a storm. They'd had them before, right? No big deal. But lightning was dangerous. She'd heard horror stories of people being struck by lightning and dying on the spot, their bodies horrifically scarred. Some said they even turned to ash. Maybe parts of it weren't true, but she didn't want to take the chance—not when just being out in that storm made the hair on her head stand straight up.

At least the rain hadn't started yet.

If Nixie had somehow called the storm to them—as crazy as that sounded to Peyton, even in her own thoughts—would she attract the lightning as well? Her body could dowse the water. Would it act as a lightning rod? The thought horrified her. She didn't want anyone in her charge getting harmed, but the thought of Nixie being struck by a bolt and her body being shocked until her skin charred made her nauseous. Still, they had to get out of this mess, get Static's parts, and get back to the riverbank. If anything of their camp was even left. With the way the wind picked up, Peyton wouldn't be surprised if nothing remained. Of course that would be just their luck.

The thunder continued to roll, and the clouds tumbled. The first drops of rain splashed down, darkening the cracked pavement. Her crew watched in awe as the single drops became a torrent.

"Well, looks like we're getting the rain we need," Jasper said dryly as he bit off a hunk of his jerky.

"Yeah, but rain this hard isn't good for the soil. It could damage the crops," Cooper argued.

"You always have to find the negative, don't you?"

"Just trying to be realistic."

"Enough, both of you. Be grateful we're getting rain at all. We need it," Peyton said, quieting them both.

Jasper put out a container to catch the rain and they continued to eat in silence. All of them stared, fixated, on the torrent. Whenever a gust of wind blew, the rain seemed to move like a wave across the pavement. Thunder continued to roll, some claps louder and longer than others. Lightning flashed across the sky, a dangerous streak against the clouds.

Peyton tried counting the seconds between strikes. If they were spaced out long enough, they could secure their packs to their backs and run like hell to the next safe point, and the next, and the next.

Trees wouldn't do, but other buildings would be okay. They'd get soaked, but considering she hadn't bathed, Peyton wouldn't mind, and from the way Static looked whenever he caught a whiff of his shirt, he wouldn't either.

"I think we can run for it," Nixie spoke up. "I've been counting the time between bolts of lightning and it's about two minutes. That should be enough for us to run to a safe place if we're quick."

Peyton stared at her. Did she somehow have the ability to read minds? No, that was impossible. But then again, with everything else she could do that seemed impossible, it wasn't as far-fetched as Peyton would have liked. But from the way Nixie returned her stare with a puzzled expression, it was just a coincidence. And then a flush raced up Nixie's cheeks and she looked away. *Ah. Well I'm not a mind reader and I know what that's from.*

That kiss.

She'd tried to push it out of her mind, to ignore it and the sensations that went along with it, but every time she looked at Nixie—when they weren't running for their lives—she thought about it. How warm her lips had been, how warm *she* had been, and how much of a comfort it was to have her near.

She does, you know. Like you.

Jasper's words came back to haunt her.

Was he right? Why did that idea appeal to her so much?

Did she really want the Scavenger having feelings for her other than respect? In general, it was a bad idea to get involved with someone when you were in charge of their well-being. That idea had been trained into her by her dad. And he was right. What if she valued Nixie's life over everyone else's? Everyone on her team had to be equal, or she'd be a terrible leader. And what if anyone else found out? Ryan would be after her job in seconds. Could she really blame him for that? No, she couldn't. Because she would do the same to him or anyone else if she found out they were favoring one of their crew over the others.

She sighed. Why was life suddenly so damned complicated?

CHAPTER TWENTY-FOUR

A s soon as the next bolt of lightning strikes, we make a run for it. Remember," Nixie said, "it's straight down this street, and then we turn right. We have less than two minutes to make it or we run the risk of being struck."

"So move your asses," Peyton added, glaring specifically at Static as she said it.

Nixie had to hide a smile as the young man gulped and stared up at their fearless leader with wide eyes. Nixie opened her mouth to say something when a flash lit up the sky outside. "Move!" she yelled instead, scrambling out of the windows and sprinting as soon as she was upright outside.

The others followed after her into the pouring rain. The water beat on her skin like tiny stinging needles, but it felt amazing. She had to force herself to keep her eyes open as she ran. In her head she tried to keep count of the seconds as they passed. The five of them raced down the street, feet pounding against the pavement and slapping in puddles. They were almost halfway to a building at the one-minute mark. *Gotta pick up the pace.*

She put on a burst of speed she hadn't known she was capable of. She hoped the others were close behind, but she wouldn't dare look for fear of losing her balance. Ninety seconds. Maybe. She lost count and swore. They would make it, right? Peyton passed her, pulling ahead as they rounded for the building. A small overhang stuck out from the side of the building closest to them and Nixie put all of her focus on it.

Just a little more. I can make it. She struggled to breathe steadily, instead of sucking in the air as quickly as possible in short bursts. Her lungs ached from the sprint and her muscles screamed in protest. Part of her considered how bad it would be, and what the chances actually were for being struck, if they were to just calmly stroll through the rain. But she didn't know the statistics. And she didn't want to risk finding out.

The building loomed before her as Cooper and Jasper passed by her nearly simultaneously. They put the brakes on moments later and avoided colliding with the brick wall. Nixie forced herself to do the same, but she wasn't as fast. Just before she hit the building with too much speed, Peyton stepped in front of her, wrapping her in strong arms. She collided with Peyton and the momentum carried them into the wall, but Peyton's body stopped her from hitting it head on. A light flashed behind her and lit up the wall.

They'd made it.

Peyton let out a grunt and Nixie immediately pulled back. "Are you okay? I should have slowed down faster."

"I'm fine," Peyton wheezed, rubbing her chest. "For someone as small as you, you pack a punch," she added lightly.

Nixie turned to survey the others and see how they'd managed. Jasper and Cooper breathed heavily, leaning against the wall. Static was doubled over with his hands on his knees. He noisily sucked in a breath, and then immediately vomited.

"Gross!" Jasper yelled, dancing away from the splatter. "Come on, man! Aim it somewhere else."

"I'm sorry," Static moaned. "I shouldn't have eaten." He retched again.

"Jazz, shut it." Peyton pushed off the wall and patted Static's back as he finished emptying his stomach on the sidewalk. "You all right?"

"I'll be fine," he said as he stood. He didn't look all right, though. His burned face looked remarkably pale and his legs and arms shook. "Just need some water."

"Well, we have plenty of that now." Nixie chuckled, trying to lighten the mood as she took out her canteen and handed it to him. Static took a careful sip, though his hands still shook.

"Where do we go from here?" Peyton asked.

Nixie looked out from the overhang and pointed. "Well, that road is the one we have to take. So we can jump to the next building and walk along it, and see what we have."

"Sounds good. Static, will be you all right if we move?"

"Yeah, it's good. I'd rather get there and rest longer than wait here." He took a deep breath and handed Nixie her canteen. "Thanks."

She smiled.

The group waited for the next bolt before sprinting the few feet between buildings. They walked along the edge of it, staying close to the sides when the roof ended just a foot or two beyond the building, but it did little to protect them from the driving rain.

Ahead of them lay an open road with no cover. Static groaned.

"Please tell me we don't have to run that, too."

"It's too far. We'd have to push just as hard as the last time, and I don't think any of us have the energy for that," Nixie said. "There are buildings on the road that runs parallel to this one. We could follow along those buildings until we come up to that one." She pointed to the large brick building in the distance. "Once we get to that one, we just have to get across the street. RadioShack is in that plaza."

"Then let's move. Again," Peyton said.

The rest just sighed.

Nixie could understand their frustration. She wanted it to be over, too. She wanted to rest and replay and analyze everything that had happened yesterday. If she hadn't been an idiot, they would have made it there and back to the river before nightfall. But then Peyton wouldn't have kissed her, and they wouldn't have this rain. But they also wouldn't be playing dodge-the-lightning-bolts.

Getting to the brick building was fairly easy. They darted between the buildings to avoid getting their packs too wet, but Nixie wondered if that was even worth it. Water ran from her hair in a steady stream and she would have loved a towel to keep her face a little dry. They waited for another clear moment before darting across the street, splashing in puddles. The large building before them stood eerily abandoned with the vacant lot before it.

"Walmart. I heard these were real big Before. You could get everything in there," Jasper said, peering through the windows. Most of them were intact, which surprised the group. Only one of the doors had been broken open.

"Should we take a look inside?" Cooper asked. "I mean, we might as well, while we're here."

"It couldn't hurt," Peyton agreed, scanning the area. "Did you check this place out?" her question was directed at Nixie.

Nixie shrugged. "I didn't. Ranger went in, but he didn't find anything of value. Wasn't in here long, though." She looked down at the ground as they stepped inside the building. A layer of dust had settled on the floor, which their footsteps disturbed.

The space was cavernous, and Nixie could only dream of what it looked like when the shelves were full. Now they stood empty and waiting, probably never to be used again.

How sad.

The group walked up and down each aisle, looking for anything useful. Most had been cleaned out. Not a scrap of food or clothing was left. In the craft aisle Nixie found a lone bucket of sidewalk chalk. She knew so many children who would love it, so she slipped it into her bag. Peyton raised an eyebrow but she just shrugged.

Everything had been stripped from the electronics section, and sports had very little left as well. Cooper squatted down at one point to examine something poking out from under a shelf and grinned triumphantly as he pulled out a package of fishing hooks.

"Well, that's certainly useful."

At the far end of the building they found a closed door that led to the gardening department. After prying the doors open, Cooper walked through to check it out with the rest following close behind.

"Damn, so many seed packets," he said as he crouched down and sorted through a knocked-over seed display. "All these are long gone now, but they would have helped a ton of people years ago."

"Wonder why they didn't take them," Nixie said softly. Jasper had wandered over to another section and picked up a pair of gardening gloves. He turned and held them up, his face triumphant.

"Probably too worried about getting food that would take care of hunger right then and there. They didn't think."

"They left some other good stuff behind, too," Jasper said from another stand. One of the shelving units had collapsed against another. "Come help me move this."

Together the five of them managed to push the unit upright once more, and Jasper's lips quirked up into a grin again. "Jackpot."

Sitting in the empty space on collapsed shelving and scattering the floor between were assorted gardening implements. Those that had been metal had rusted to some degree—some more than others—but the plastic pieces appeared to be in excellent shape. Coiled lengths of hose piled on top of each other.

"Well...it will be heavy to carry back, but I don't see why we can't take some of it. As long as we leave Static free to carry his parts," Peyton said as she hefted one of the coils.

"Whatever we don't grab, we can always come back for, now that we know it's here," Cooper added. "If we need it, anyway."

The four of them took off their packs loaded some of the supplies in. With the exception of their food and water canteens they were mostly empty because of the supplies left at the campsite. As they worked, Peyton reminded them to leave room for the tents and blankets.

In the end they had to leave a lot behind, but Cooper marked the place on his map. They wandered back out into the main part of the building where the heavy rain thundered on the roof.

"Man, it would be nice if the rain would let up for just a few minutes," Jasper said as they peered out into the storm from the smashed door.

"Well it's not, so let's just go," Peyton said, and they ran out, darting once more down the broken sidewalks.

RadioShack sat farther down the line of the shops. Cooper insisted they peek inside each one, just to be safe, but from the front windows they could tell nothing remained. They'd just gotten extremely lucky at Walmart.

"I don't see anything. What if there's nothing there?" Static asked, his fidgeting returning as they finally neared the building. He clasped his hands together, wringing them as if they held a wet towel.

"Then there's nothing we can do about it. It was a chance we took when we decided to make this trip, but at least we'll know. Come on."

The windows of RadioShack were intact, but like the rest, the front door had been broken open. Carefully they stepped inside, the glass crunching under their feet. Static let out a whimper. The shelves and hooks on the walls were empty and the cash register had been broken open on the floor, the innards spilling out in a mess of wires. Some boxes and packaging remained on the floor, but when Cooper went over to investigate, he looked back and shook his head. "They're empty."

Static didn't say a word, but he didn't have to. Nixie watched his shoulders slump and his head hang low. Whatever had been driving him to keep going had fled, and he sank down onto the ground. Nixie worried for a moment about the glass, but then saw that he was beyond reach of the shards.

"Hey," she said as she slid up to him and placed a hand on his back. He shuddered with each breath and Nixie worried he'd freak out right there. "We'll find another place that has what you need. This can't be the only RadioShack."

"The others were probably raided a long time ago, too," he said miserably. He brought a hand up and rubbed at his face just as Cooper called from the back of the store.

"Hey. This door back here is locked. Someone come help me."

Nixie looked up to see him standing at a door that she would have missed if she hadn't been looking for it. Cooper had latched onto the handle and shook it violently, but it didn't budge.

"Let me try," Jasper said. He dropped his pack to the ground and rummaged through the front pockets a minute before producing a small toolkit.

"What's that?" Nixie asked, curious as to what he would need it for.

"A skill I picked up when I was younger. Back when I was still training to be a guard," he said as he shuffled on his knees to get closer to the handle, "we sometimes went to places that were locked up tight. One of the other guards showed me how to pick a lock and get in."

"Why not just break the door down?"

"Sometimes you can't do that. Besides. It's not always bad to leave a door locked. It deters most people because there are easier places to get into. Okay, I need quiet now."

Nixie couldn't tell what he was doing. He stared at the lock for a bit, and then went back to his toolkit and produced two small tools. The four of them watched as he stuck them both in the lock and started wiggling things around. He had closed both of his eyes and had his head tilted so that he could listen to whatever he was doing.

In the entire time it took him to pick the lock, Nixie could scarcely breathe. Static must have been holding his breath as well, because his face took on a dark shade of red, and his hands were clenched so tightly they turned white.

"Got it!" Jasper exclaimed as he twisted one of the tools. He reached up and turned the handle and it swung open with a gentle squeal. "Makes you wonder about their security Before Collapse."

As Jasper returned his tools to their correct place, Static jumped to his feet. Cooper was the first through the door. "Damn."

CHAPTER TWENTY-FIVE

Static pushed past him, nearly knocking him over, and cried out.

Peyton peered into the room, looking beyond Cooper's broad shoulders to find a large back room. It had apparently been part stockroom and part office. To one side a series of workstations and desks took up a wall, with a table jutting out and chairs placed around it. A refrigerator took up space against another wall. Some paperwork littered one of the desks as if waiting for the boss to get back.

"It's like time just stopped for this side of the room," Nixie said in awe. Cooper let both of them through and Peyton could see that the other half was just as abandoned but empty.

A metal cage of sorts took up another section, the gated door wide open. Static had hooked his fingers through the chain links, and he stared into the space with a forlorn look on his face.

Cooper walked deeper into the stockroom and rummaged around on the desk, pushing papers out of the way. He pulled open the drawers and sorted through them.

"Hey. Check this out."

Peyton glanced over. He held up a small box. "What is it?"

"Hell if I know. Static might though."

Peyton placed a hand on his shoulder. "Static, you should go look. Maybe it'll be helpful."

Static let out a sigh and shuffled over to Cooper. Together they sifted through the contents of the box. As they worked, Static's energy returned and he started ripping through the other drawers.

"What is it?" Peyton asked.

"This stuff…I can make it work!" He turned to look at them, a feverish look in his eyes. "It's not exactly what I need, but I can adapt the parts. I'll need some different wiring, but I can cannibalize parts from…"

"What's he talking about?" Nixie whispered.

"I have no idea. But I think he found what he needs." Peyton watched as he sifted through the materials, stripping smaller components from larger pieces he discarded. The change in him was night and day. Static had never been one who seemed in control, but this was his element.

"Hey," Nixie called after a moment. Peyton turned to find her in a corner, rummaging through boxes. "We were supposed to grab plastic bags, right? Because I think I found everything we need." Sure enough, she'd found a box filled with black plastic bags.

"Perfect," Static said. "We can use the bags to wrap each part individually. It will protect them from being jostled around and breaking, and from the rain. Two birds with one stone." His entire face lit up when he spoke, and he instructed Cooper to get the bags. Cooper glanced at Peyton, who just shrugged. *He's in charge now. Just roll with it. I'm so far out of my league.*

Half an hour passed with Static barking out his orders, packing the electronic components—he wouldn't let anyone else do it—and setting them carefully in his pack. When he finished, he struggled to shoulder the bag. His face had turned pale again and he looked exhausted. It seemed like getting sick earlier was catching up to him after his rapid changes in emotion.

"If you get tired, I'll carry it," Cooper offered. Static opened his mouth and looked like he would outright reject the offer, but Peyton stopped him.

"That's a great idea. We'll all take turns. We're in this together as a team, right?" They all murmured their agreement. "Good. Let's head out."

When they left RadioShack, the storm had slowed. The rain came down in a steady drizzle. It was enough to keep them wet and Static worried aloud about his electronics, but as a whole they were able to move between buildings and trees.

Cooper had mapped out a new route back to the riverbank now that they knew where they were. It would take a lot less time, and with any luck, they'd be back well before nightfall. Peyton was eager to get back to the Mill, and if it had been just her and one other person, she wouldn't have minded traveling at night. It wasn't safe, especially without the moon shining and lighting their path. They'd spend one more night on the river and then make the trek back to the Mill.

Jasper took the lead with Cooper this time, with Static trailing behind them, shifting the pack from shoulder to shoulder. Peyton watched over him to make sure he didn't trip, but for once he seemed completely attentive and aware of his footfalls. Nixie walked next to her, keeping pace. Aside from the boys' chattering, it was quiet, but Peyton knew that wouldn't last. She could see Nixie turning to look at her from the corner of her eye, and every time Peyton turned to address her, she'd whipped her head back around to face front.

They needed to talk about the kiss before they got back. She didn't want any misunderstandings between them. She'd just done it to shut Nixie up. Of course. Any logical person would have done it if the person in question was freaking out.

Dad would have done it for Graham.

But she needed to be honest, at least with herself: Shutting Nixie up might have been the reason she'd done it initially, but it had transformed into so much more the moment their lips had touched. She could deny that all she wanted to everyone else, but not to herself. The kiss was magic, and it left her reeling.

"Umm…" the soft voice came from her side. Peyton braced herself as she turned to look at Nixie and finally caught her gaze. "About yesterday and what happened. In the alley."

Peyton hesitated, but her heartbeat galloped. "What about it?"

"Why did you kiss me?"

Tell her the truth. "I did it to shut you up."

Tell her the whole truth. "You were hysterical and there was nothing else I could think of that would work. I did try talking to you, but you just kept going."

Coward! Tell her it was more than that.

"So you kissed me."

"Yup."

"No one's ever kissed me before." Nixie's voice was soft, and Peyton looked over at her, startled. Her lips had turned up in a soft smile, her eyes unfocused on the ground. Looking, but not seeing.

"I didn't mean anything by it," Peyton said quickly. The words came out harsh, much harsher than she'd intended, and she winced at her own tone.

No! That's not what she meant. That was all wrong.

When she looked at Nixie to take it back, though, she realized she didn't have to. Either Nixie hadn't heard or she didn't believe her, because the serene look on her face made her practically glow.

The heat rose in Peyton's cheeks and spread down her neck. She raised an arm and scratched at the back of her head, trying to cover up. She was completely out of her depth with this situation, and she was sinking.

Fast.

CHAPTER TWENTY-SIX

Peyton tried so hard to be tough, but Nixie finally had figured her out. She couldn't keep the smile from her face as Peyton floundered, trying to come up with something to cover her tracks. Even the harsh declaration hadn't bothered Nixie. Silence fell between them again and the boys picked up their pace. The sun fell closer to the horizon, but they would make it back to their site in time.

As the boys turned a corner and disappeared from view, Nixie shuffled a step closer to her and slid her small hand into Peyton's. Peyton's fingers closed around hers reflexively as Peyton let out a small noise—not quite a gasp, but not a grunt either—and then the grip loosened. Nixie twisted her fingers so they slid between Peyton's and the noise turned into a soft sigh.

Peyton's skin was calloused as if she were a farmer or a forager and not a guard. But despite the roughness, or maybe because of it, it felt good to hold on to her. The heat from her palm soaked into Nixie's and she allowed herself to close her eyes for a brief moment. It felt so good to be close to another person. That kiss Peyton had given her made Nixie realize how much she missed the contact. It had been pleasurable but also incredibly painful. She hadn't realized how alone she was, and now it brought her face-to-face with the harsh reality. When the guard didn't pull her hand away, Nixie breathed a sigh of relief. It was faint, but Peyton must have heard because she chuckled. A small wave of embarrassment flooded through her body, but she forced it back. There was no reason to be embarrassed.

They turned the corner, still hand in hand. The boys had gotten farther ahead, and they continued to follow at an almost leisurely pace, as though they had all the time in the world. And Nixie wished they did. It would be nice to spend time getting to know Peyton without having to worry about anything else.

Nixie hadn't realized how much taller Peyton was. Even when they'd kissed—or rather, when Peyton had kissed her and she'd stood there too stupid to respond—she hadn't registered their difference in height. Now as she held her hand, the difference was hard to ignore. The top of Nixie's head barely made it to Peyton's shoulder as they walked. In fact, if she were to turn her head right now, she'd smack her nose right against Peyton's upper arm.

Funny how they didn't have to say anything. Nixie didn't feel the need to. She was content to walk next to her, holding her hand. Around them, the cityscape decayed with buildings slowly collapsing and roadways crumbling. Through the cracks in the concrete plants sprang, and even though their creations fell, humans continued to grow stronger.

By the time they arrived at the river, the sun had kissed the horizon. Peyton gradually pulled her hand away from Nixie's, and while she mourned the loss, she was glad she hadn't snatched her hand back quickly. Static had already placed his pack down on a dry patch of land under a tree and worked at stretching his back.

"Well, at least the damage isn't that bad," Peyton said as she surveyed their campsite.

A few branches had fallen from the storm, knocking over the gear they had set up around the fire pit. Their dry wood was soaked and scattered around. Both tents had been ripped out of the ground but lay only a few dozen feet away, caught against a copse of trees. Cooper and Jasper worked at untangling them and managed to get them out.

"How are the tents?" Peyton asked as she righted the rest of their gear. Nixie set to work removing branches from the fire pit. After storing his things, Static ran over to help her.

Jasper spread out one of the tents and staked it into the ground. "This one looks fine," he said, running his hands down the sides, taking care at the seams. "Yup, nothing."

"This one has a tear at the seam," Cooper said, indicating the tent Nixie shared with Peyton. She frowned and glanced over to see where the side had ripped open near one of the poles. "It'll be fine for tonight, though. When we get back to the Mill it can be patched up."

"Just hope it doesn't rain," Peyton said, shooting Nixie a glance.

"We'll put you under the trees and hope they don't fall on you," Jasper teased. He glanced up at the branches, selected a spot, and then helped Cooper stake the tent down.

By the time the sun had dipped below the horizon, Cooper had managed to get a weak fire going. He kept his attention on it while the rest of them scrounged for wood that would be dry enough. Nixie managed to find a few branches under the bridge that had escaped their notice the first time around and brought those back.

Their food supply had dwindled, and Nixie was glad they were heading back in the morning. Even though Cooper could find food, and she had gone without or with little for days at a time before, now that she'd had steady meals she didn't want to give it up. She was getting too comfortable. If she went back, it would be hard to adjust.

The thought stopped her short.

Since when was it *if* she went back?

The group hardly spoke during their meal, too exhausted to do much more than chew and swallow. Nixie watched them all, and though they looked weary, the atmosphere was not tense. When Peyton announced she would take first watch, Jasper merely nodded agreement and crawled to his tent. Cooper followed moments later. Static lasted a little longer, going through his pack methodically and murmuring softly to himself as he looked at each component. Nixie had no idea how he would make the mess of parts and wires work, but it wasn't her place to judge. Eventually he, too, followed his friends into their tent and sealed it shut.

With him gone, Nixie moved closer to Peyton so they could talk in quiet tones and not risk the others hearing. Her side pressed against Peyton's side and that was an added bonus.

"When I found you this morning," Peyton started, "you were in a trance. You were dancing and completely unaware of anything."

"It's hard for me to remember what happened. Bits and pieces are coming to me. I remember waking up, and then I remember you shaking me, and the thunder."

"You didn't know you could do that?" Peyton asked, her eyes boring into Nixie as if she could see into her soul.

"No," she insisted, with a shake of her head. "I've never done anything like that before. I almost don't want to believe it."

"Why not? It's an incredible gift."

Nixie sighed. "That's the problem. It is a gift, and if I've had it all this time, and people have suffered because I didn't use it…" She let her words trail off in frustration. If all of this was true, and she had the ability to call the rain, she could have helped her people a long time ago. She could have helped *all* people. She could have kept the Settlers' crops from failing. Kept Mrs. Burgoine's from burning. She could have kept the water levels high. So many *could-have*s.

Peyton reached out and brushed her palm against Nixie's cheek. She gently turned her face so they were looking at each other.

"You didn't know."

"How could I *not* know?"

"How could you?" Peyton asked in response, and she was right. How could Nixie have known?

She closed her eyes, trying to block out all other sensations to tune into her body and see if it felt different, but she couldn't concentrate with the warmth from Peyton's hand distracting her. When she opened her eyes again, Peyton had drawn closer, the warmth in her hand reflected in her eyes. They hadn't known each other long, but Nixie hadn't seen a look like that from her before. It was warm. Comforting. And only a little bit wistful.

CHAPTER TWENTY-SEVEN

Peyton couldn't pinpoint when she'd decided to allow herself to get closer to Nixie, and maybe she hadn't exactly made the decision herself. Maybe it had just happened. That was okay, because the water witch had gotten under her skin in a good way and if that didn't tell her something, she didn't know what did. Without hesitating, she leaned forward, closing the distance between them and pressed her lips against Nixie's. This time she responded instantly instead of remaining frozen.

Her lips were cool, refreshing, like a summer rain on a blistering day. They were softer and fuller this time around. It was as if her body had absorbed the water from the rainstorm. Hell, maybe it did. At this point she wouldn't be surprised if Nixie could jump into a lake and drink without ever opening her mouth.

Nixie worked her slender arms around her shoulders. She knew she should be keeping watch, and she tried to keep her senses open to more than just Nixie. But the girl in her arms was intoxicating, heady stuff. It was hard to focus when their mouths opened, tongues tangling, and breaths coming together in soft, shared puffs.

In the end, she broke the kiss just as she had been the one to initiate it. Nixie looked at her through half-lidded eyes, dazed. "You should get some sleep," Peyton said, and her voice came out hoarse.

Nixie didn't say anything, just nodded as she stood and staggered off to their tent as if drunk. Peyton bit back a chuckle at the sight.

Without Nixie at her side, the night passed slowly. She kept stirring the flames of the fire, adding a log when needed. All around her the crickets sang louder than she had ever heard, and Peyton thought that perhaps the rain had refreshed them as well. Had it rained back at the Mill? She hoped so, because they needed it. She wished she had been there to see the look on their faces as lightning split the sky in two and rain beat down on them. She hoped no one had been injured.

That thought gave her pause.

What if someone had been caught out, unable to find shelter or make it back? Maybe they had time, seen the clouds coming in the distance. Peyton and her group hadn't had that luxury because the storm had started where they were, a product of Nixie's skills. It was pointless to worry about it now. She couldn't do anything about it, even if someone had been injured. They were too far away, and some things were simply beyond her control.

Like Dad's death.

She sighed as the words came unbidden to the surface. It had been a little over a month since he'd been killed, and the pain still hit her as if it had happened yesterday. Every time she thought of him, the wound ripped back open. He wouldn't want her to be consumed by it, and really, she wasn't. Still, whenever she thought of him, the pain bloomed deep in her chest and spread outward until she burned with it. And eventually that burn turned to anger, a slow anger that threatened to consume her.

She thought back to that day they'd buried him and her promise to find who'd killed him and punish them. When she'd asked Nixie about the Scavengers who murdered her father, she claimed not to know. Peyton hadn't wanted to trust her at first, but now she did. Nixie didn't know who killed him, but what if it was someone close to her that held the secret? Would Peyton want to be responsible for taking the light out of those blue eyes and putting sorrow there?

Not if she could help it.

Her mind raced as the moon crept across the sky. How would she punish his murderers? She'd been so sure that she would bring them back to the Mill and execute them. She'd wanted revenge so badly she had been able to taste the blood…but now she'd lost the taste for it. Revenge wouldn't bring her father back. What was the point?

Maybe Jasper was right. She was soft on Nixie, and she was getting soft on everyone else. Times were changing. A few months ago she would have balked at the idea, but now it didn't seem so bad. *With Nixie at my side, I feel like I can do anything.*

Wasn't that just a kicker?

The boys' tent rustled and the sound of a zipper broke the stillness of the evening.

Speak of the devil. Peyton watched Jasper as he crawled slowly and carefully from the tent, doing his best not to disturb Cooper and Static. He stretched and yawned, his back popping loudly as he stood.

"Didn't realize you were getting so ancient, old man," Peyton teased quietly as he approached her place. He flipped her off as he sat down.

"You should hear yourself, then." He stared into the flames, his eyes slipping closed for a moment.

"If you're still tired, you should sleep longer. I can manage a few more hours." Even if she went to bed now, she didn't think she'd be able to sleep. Not with Nixie so close.

"Nah, I'm good," Jasper said, waving a hand in her direction. "It's just one more night, right? I'll manage."

"We both deserve a day of rest after this trip."

"You said it. I say Ryan takes my shifts." His grin showed his teeth, the white catching the fire and reflecting back dangerously. Peyton chuckled.

"Somehow I doubt that'll go over well."

"You're the boss. Just make him do it."

Peyton shrugged a shoulder and stood, stretching her back as she did. "I could. We'll see." She wouldn't. As much as she couldn't stand Ryan, she knew dumping Jasper's load on him would do more harm than the momentary pleasure of watching him work a double shift. Retaliation on Ryan's part would likely hurt an innocent, and she couldn't allow that to happen.

Quietly she bid Jasper good night and slipped over to her tent. Nixie hadn't zipped it fully, so she pulled the zipper enough to let her crawl through before turning and sealing them in. Two sleeping mats lay on the floor—one for her, and one for Nixie. But in her sleep, Nixie must have moved around because she was in the center, occupying half of both mats.

Peyton sighed softly and sat on the ground, carefully removing her boots and placing them off to the side. She eased onto her side, back to Nixie, and tried to settle into a comfortable position. It was hard to with Nixie taking up so much space. Amazing how someone so small could fill a room or a tent.

Nixie murmured in her sleep and shifted, scooting back a little so that her back pressed against Peyton's. Peyton held her breath, not wanting to wake her. She was afraid to wake her. Afraid of what she'd do if she looked into those drowsy, trusting eyes.

Half on her mat, half on the hard ground, Peyton closed her eyes and tried to sleep. The heat radiating from Nixie's body warmed her and lulled her into a peaceful rest, but she didn't sleep. Her body might be comforted by the nearness, but her mind just wouldn't shut off.

"I can hear you thinking," Nixie murmured sleepily.

Peyton nearly ripped a hole in the tent when she flailed out in surprise. "What are you doing awake?" she asked. Then she added, "Move over, you left me no room."

"That was the point," Nixie said. Her voice sounded more alert this time, the sleep fading with each word. The blanket rustled as she shifted, and Peyton rolled onto her back. She glanced over to find herself face-to-face with Nixie.

"The point?"

Nixie shook her head and slid back on her mat. Peyton took the opportunity to settle more fully onto her own, but before she finished, a small arm wrapped around her waist and a head came down to rest on her shoulder. She stiffened, surprised by the contact. Nixie's breathing evened out again, and Peyton was stuck in her position, comfortable or not.

It's going to be a long night.

CHAPTER TWENTY-EIGHT

The sun shone brightly the next morning as they set out for the Mill. All of their gear had been packed, a hasty breakfast eaten, and more water filtered to fill their canteens. Static waved good-bye to the campsite, calling out, "Fare thee well!" as they crossed the bridge. Everyone laughed.

"I've never seen him acting so strange," Cooper said.

Static grinned, the color rising in his cheeks from a blush rather than a burn. "Just glad to be going back to get started on my work," he replied.

They were all glad to be returning, Nixie decided. Jasper teased Static, watching him carefully as they walked over the cracked highway. Cooper wandered off to explore, bringing back various plant samples or edibles and marking their location on his map. And Peyton...Peyton had a small smile that actually reached her eyes, and she flashed it to Nixie every so often.

It lit her up like a clear, starry night.

Everything felt so easy. The tension from their trip out had faded and was replaced with a pleasant camaraderie in which Nixie felt included. Whether it was from the success of their mission, the landscape, fresh and bright from the rain, or something else entirely, Nixie couldn't tell. On the first trip, the group had walked in a mostly single-file row with Jasper and Peyton constantly on the alert, scanning their surroundings and switching places seamlessly. Now the group walked nearly side-by-side. Jasper and Peyton still scanned their surroundings, but hard lines didn't mar their faces, and their eyes were wide open and bright instead of narrowed. Peyton walked next to Nixie most of the time, too, and didn't try to keep her voice whisper quiet when she spoke.

For the first time in her life, Nixie felt as if she were a valuable part of the mission instead of just an accessory added on after the fact.

It gave her an idea.

"Peyton," she said after a long stretch of silence between them. The girl looked at her, eyebrow raised, as she grunted acknowledgment of her name. "If Scavengers were to show up at the Mill, in peace, wanting to join the settlement, would they be accepted?" Despite the progress between them and their shared kisses, Nixie half expected the guard to recoil, so she was surprised when Peyton took her question seriously and gave it careful consideration. She didn't answer right away, and after ticking off the seconds in her head, Nixie wondered if she had dismissed the idea and wasn't going to bother with an answer.

"I'm not sure, honestly," Peyton said finally. "I'd like to say they'd be welcomed, but I think a lot of people would have problems with it, for a lot of reasons, not just because they're Scavengers." She carefully picked her way over a clump of concrete before continuing. "There would be a lot of distrust at first. People would want to know why they were there. They'd think they were after something, like you were."

Nixie felt the color rising in her face. Had she ruined her people's chance at a better life?

"But after this mission, some might change their minds. Avery certainly likes you, and if Avery does, Julian will. Graham trusts you, and Dr. Easton. If you can get Old Joe's approval, then it will make the rest of the people easier." She paused before adding, "And then there's us, of course." Her smile chased the worry from Nixie's gut. "It would take a while, but I think it can be done. Of course there are other issues as well. Where would they stay? What would we do about food? Clothing? It would be taxing on our resources, at least initially, depending on how many people came for help. But I think in the long run, it would only make us stronger. And with Static trying to connect us with the rest of the country, shouldn't we be doing that?"

"Have you been thinking about this?" Nixie asked.

Peyton shrugged. "It might have crossed my mind. Do you think there are Scavengers who would try?"

"If I talked to them, yes. I think there are some who would. I know they'd at least consider it." She shook her head sadly. "Life as a Scavenger is hard. Not everyone is made for it, and I know the mothers worry about their children. Just the thought of a solid roof over their heads and more food in their bellies would be enough for some."

"Were you hungry growing up?"

The hunger pangs still haunted Nixie, and she closed her eyes, remembering nights when she'd stumbled across berries she was told never to eat, and the temptation to pluck them from their branches just to ease the gnawing hunger had grown so strong she'd almost given in the way some had. She'd seen adults and children cave in. It didn't happen often, but when it did, the loss lay over the group like a swarm of bees. And then the guilt seeped in, because someone, usually a family member, would benefit from the extra rations. While they mourned the loss of their loved one, they greedily ate their share of the food, their constant hunger temporarily abated as rations increased. The irony of it all was lost on no one.

She realized she hadn't answered the question, but when she looked at Peyton, she knew she didn't have to. The answer must've been written all over her face.

"If you stay with us, you'll never have to feel that way again."

"I know."

The group stopped a little after noon to eat the rest of their food. Nixie would have been worried if they weren't on their way back to the Mill, or if Cooper hadn't been with them. But shortly after eating, and during a brief rest for Static's benefit, the forager had wandered off and came back with a plastic bag full of greens.

Jasper laughed at the sight of him strolling back through the brush. "You look like you've just gone to the grocery store."

"I wish it were that easy," Cooper said as he set the bag on the ground. They crowded around and looked inside. "It's peppergrass. I figured we could snack on some of it and give the rest to Mrs. Burgoine on our way back, when we drop off her bags."

Peyton murmured her agreement and after they had picked through a few of the leaves, the group resumed their progress. Time passed quickly as they headed into familiar territory for all of them. The group picked up their pace, and soon the recognizable sites passed faster than they had on the first trip. Nixie commented on it, and Jasper said it was because they were all eager to get home.

By late afternoon, they reached Ox Farm. The little girl was nowhere to be seen, but the chickens were picking at the ground in an enclosed yard. Out in the field Nixie saw two large men working with large, handheld tools. As they approached the farmhouse a dog barked and growled from inside.

"Hello?" Peyton called out. Nixie glanced through the screen and could see a large brown dog baring its teeth. Peyton didn't bother knocking on the screen, though she held up her hands, palm out to the dog. It seemed to pacify it for the moment.

"Yes?" a voice called from around the back of the house. Nixie poked her head around the corner to find Mrs. Burgoine walking toward them, her hair pulled back into a ponytail. Little Ada trailed after her, holding a basket. "Oh! You're back already! I thought you would have been gone much longer."

"We would have been back yesterday, but we got a little lost in the city. We found the bags you requested."

Everyone unloaded the bags and Mrs. Burgoine exclaimed in delight. She took them gratefully, along with the bag of peppergrass from Cooper. "So many bags! This will keep us for a long time. Thank you!"

"We found them in RadioShack with the parts Static needed."

"So you found everything?"

Static grinned and turned to show off the bulging pack he carried.

"That's amazing. I wouldn't have thought anything would be left."

"Well…technically there wasn't much. But I can adapt what we found. I—"

"Makes you wonder what else is there," Nixie said, cutting Static off before he could get going.

"Maybe all the settlements can group together and send in a larger party. It couldn't hurt," Mrs. Burgoine said.

Everyone turned to Peyton and she nodded slowly. "I think it's time we start exploring again."

"We need to do it sometime. No time like the present," Mrs. Burgoine added. "Thank you again for the bags. If you have anything you need repaired, send it over and I'd be happy to mend it for you."

"Thank you," Jasper said. "I think we do have some damaged netting. Willow mentioned something about it."

"Oh! The strangest thing happened after you passed through. You'll probably hear about it from your people, but it rained!"

"Rain, rain, rain!" Ada sang, setting her basket down and skipping about the yard. "Thunder and lightning, rain!"

"The storm came out of nowhere and didn't last nearly long enough, but it was so refreshing. It gave us hope. Maybe the climate is changing." She trailed off with a sigh. "Did it rain in the city?"

"Yes, just as you said. Sudden and intense."

"Well, I hope it comes again." Mrs. Burgoine looked up at the clear blue sky. "Though, right now, it doesn't look like it."

"You never know," Nixie spoke up. "The sky looked like this before it started to rain, right?"

The woman gave her an appraising glance before nodding. "Yes, you're right."

Before they left, Mrs. Burgoine insisted on filling their canteens. She asked Nixie to help her, so she followed along while the others rested outside.

"I don't know everyone at the Mill, but I get this feeling that you're new there."

The question would have caused panic on the trip out to the city, but a lot had happened since then, and Nixie just handed over another canteen. "You're right. I am new. I'm from the area, but I've only been at the Mill for a few months."

"Good to know my instincts are still strong." She laughed.

Nixie stilled her pounding heart as best she could, then added, "I'm a Scavenger."

The hand turning on the faucet to fill the last canteen paused. Mrs. Burgoine stared at the sink for a moment before turning to Nixie with a look of surprise. "Well, I'll be."

"You'll be what?"

"Just an old expression. My grandmother used to say it when she was surprised." She finished the job and tightened the cap. She didn't make another comment on the matter as they left the house and rejoined the group lounging outside.

"Thanks for the water, Mrs. Burgoine," Peyton said as she took hers back. She hooked it onto her pack and stood.

"Anytime. Thanks again for your help," the woman said with a smile. She nodded at Nixie and called for Ada. They all parted ways with friendly waves and Ada chasing after them, laughing and singing about the rain.

Nixie watched the little girl until they disappeared around the bend and hoped her new ability wasn't just a one-time fluke.

CHAPTER TWENTY-NINE

Going into the city, they had come down the steep part of West Street, but on the return trip, they had to climb it. Static, who had been pleasant until this point, complained as soon as they hit the base, and Jasper traded packs with him.

"I can't wait to be home," he moaned, trudging up the hill. "I have blisters on my feet. There are blisters on my blisters."

"We're all tired, Static, so shut up," Cooper grumbled. "It's not going to make this any easier or faster."

"But it feels good to get it out," he whined.

"It won't feel good when I knock you out."

"Enough, boys." Peyton's command stopped them for a moment, but the silence didn't last long. Peyton wished she had something to tie Static's mouth shut, at least for the last leg of their journey. At her side, Nixie snickered, and the boys were quiet for all of five minutes before they started up again. Peyton tried to ignore them and instead focused on thoughts of home and her own bed. A softer bed than the ground she'd been sleeping on.

Maybe Nixie would want to move into my place.

She didn't need a mirror to show her the color rising in her cheeks; she could feel it from the thoughts and images that flitted through her mind. *Maybe she'd rather stay with Graham.* Once the group crested the rise of the hill, it was all downhill back to the Mill. They picked up their pace and Static's complaints turned to exclamations of how everyone would throw a parade in his honor once he got the radios back up and working.

"What's a parade?" Nixie murmured by her side.

"Something that involves marching down roads," she responded with a vague shrug. She'd either read about it once or heard about it from someone who lived Before, but it didn't affect her now, so she couldn't bring herself to be interested.

"Why would someone want that?"

"No idea."

People were working outside when they finally reached the Mill. Static waved at everyone as he passed. They stared at him for a moment, likely in surprise, before waving back. Willow approached them from one of the fields.

"You know, with how much we keep seeing you with the farmers, maybe you should consider a career change," Jasper teased.

Willow rolled her eyes and swatted at him. "Shut it. From the look on Static's face, I take it he found what he needed?"

"More or less," Peyton replied. Static didn't hold the door open for them, and while it grated on her nerves, she let him go. He was home and eager to get started. Any delay would just push his sanity over the edge. "How's everything been here?" she asked, taking her pack off and stretching her arms and back. The others followed suit, and Nixie instantly dropped to the ground. She'd held up well during the trip and, despite her small frame, carried her share of the load. She would make a great asset to the Mill. In more ways than one…

Peyton couldn't fight the fond smile that split her face, so she didn't bother trying. Let the others see it. She was home, tired, and maybe just a little bit falling in love.

Nixie suddenly jerked her head around and looked up at Peyton and Willow.

Shit. Did I just say that out loud?

"Peyton?"

Willow had been talking, and she'd missed everything, completely lost in her own thoughts. She frowned, wondering what had Nixie falling so pale. She turned to Willow and focused. "What did you say?"

"I said we caught another Scavenger trying to break in. Well, Ryan did and he won't stop gloating about it. I think it's the same one that tried to get in a few weeks ago, after the first break-in."

"A Scavenger tried to get in after—"

"Where is he?" Peyton said, cutting Nixie off. She didn't want to get into it, not when things had been going so well.

"Ryan? He's probably with the Scav. We put him where we kept her," Willow said, gesturing toward Nixie.

"Her name is Nixie," Peyton and Jasper said simultaneously. They looked at each other and Jasper cracked a smile.

"Who is it?" Nixie demanded.

"Dunno. He never gave his name, no matter how much Ryan tried to beat it out of him. Not that I agreed with what he was doing, but you know how Ryan can—"

Peyton groaned as Nixie took off down the hallway to the stairs that led to the basement. She quickly dismissed Cooper and followed after her, with Jasper and Willow on her heels. Before they even got to the room, Peyton heard Ryan through the door. Nixie was ahead of them and she barely stopped long enough to wrench the door open before darting inside. Peyton followed.

At first Peyton couldn't process the scene before her. A man lay bound on the floor with Ryan standing over him. Ryan turned, his lips pulled back in a triumphant, almost feral grin.

"Ryan," she said, her voice nearly inaudible. "What did you do?"

Nixie cried out, "Ranger!" and rushed to the man's side. She dropped down to the man, placing herself between him and Ryan. "Are you okay?"

Ranger opened one eye and grunted. "Nixie. You're okay. I didn't think you'd made it. This bastard didn't tell me anything."

"Watch your words, Scav, or I'll beat—"

"Ryan, that's enough. Get out." Ryan turned to face Peyton. She narrowed her eyes and stepped forward.

"I'm not leaving. You weren't here for us when we needed you, and I did the job. You don't deserve your position."

"Now is not the time for arguing. We can talk about that later, but right now we need Dr. Easton. Does she know about this?"

"The good doctor was called away to Ellington yesterday." His lips kicked up at the corners in a cruel smirk, and his eyes flashed dangerously even in the dim light.

"Jasper, get Graham." Her friend nodded and bolted through the door, leaving Peyton staring down Ryan with Willow at her side. She could hear the murmured conversation behind her, but some of the words were lost in the quiet.

Nixie sat in front of Ranger, still in shock at seeing him in such terrible condition. Half of his face had disappeared under crusted blood, with a range of cuts still seeping. His bottom lip had split while his left eye had swollen shut. His arms were bound to his sides with a thick rope that crossed over his chest, and his wrists had been tied behind his back. Nixie moved carefully behind him and gently ran a hand down his arm to find the knot and work at it.

"What happened?" she asked softly, not wanting the others to overhear.

"Faulkner sent me to retrieve you. We were almost caught the first time so I needed to re-strategize, but clearly that didn't work," he said wryly. "We need you. I came back alone—figured it would be easier with just me this time, and if this happened, no one else would be at risk."

"I didn't know you came back before. They didn't tell me."

"Why would they? I wanted to come back even sooner than this, but Faulkner didn't want to risk it. Said you'd be fine. Guess he was right."

"I'm okay now, but a month is a long time."

"I should have tried sooner. We should have had a contingency plan in case someone was taken in the first place. I'm sorry."

"Don't apologize. I don't need it. Let's get you out of here and cleaned up."

The knot loosened and Nixie carefully pulled the loops, slipping it free of his hands once it was loose enough. She moved to the knot at his back as he flexed his wrists.

"They treatin' you all right?"

"There not bad people," she said softly, flicking her glance up at Peyton who squared off with Ryan. "I trust them."

"They're the same people who kept you here."

"I know," Nixie said, frustrated. How could she make him understand that things—people—change? "It's more complicated than that. Just trust me on this, okay? Would I ever lead you wrong?"

Ranger sighed and dropped his head forward. With her small fingers she worked at the last knot until it loosened and fell away. Ranger sucked in a deep breath. "Thank God. I thought I'd never get out."

"How long have you been here?"

"Day? Maybe two? I lost track of time. I think I lost consciousness at one point."

Nixie looked over to the others. "Peyton? He needs to see Dr. Easton. He's hurt bad."

"Dr. Easton isn't here, but we'll do what we can until she's back," Peyton said. She turned back to Ryan as the door opened and Jasper strode in with Graham.

"We need to move him to Doc's suite," Peyton instructed. Jasper and Willow moved forward to help lift Ranger, who pulled away from them.

"Dude, it's cool. We've got you," Jasper said. He held out a hand as one would to a scared dog. Ranger hesitated before nodding and letting the smaller man help him stand. "We're not like that one," he added, jerking his chin toward Ryan.

"Did you know about this, Graham?" Peyton asked as they led Ranger from his prison. Nixie stood torn. Part of her wanted to stay with Peyton, hear what Graham had to stay, and help, but the other part wanted to go with Ranger and make him feel safe. In the end, her concern for Ranger won out, and she closed the door behind her.

CHAPTER THIRTY

D id you know about this?" Peyton demanded again, once the door shut and cut them off from Nixie. Graham stood before her with his hands shoved in his pockets. "Did you know he was keeping someone down here?"

"Someone? He's a Scav," Ryan said.

"He's still a person!" she yelled. Back and forth she paced, gesturing as she spoke. It was that, or her fists would make their marks on Ryan's smug face.

"Touchy. Since when did you get so friendly with them? Don't tell me you've got a soft spot for that little one."

What could a few rounds hurt? She turned on him as one of Graham's warm hands landed on her shoulder and pulled her back with a strength she'd forgotten he had.

"Peyton, don't. Don't let him push you."

"You still didn't answer my question."

"I knew."

She backed away from his hand, the words an arrow through her chest. "You knew?"

Graham sighed and ran the same hand that had been on her shoulder over his face. "I knew he'd been caught breaking in. I didn't know what Ryan had done with him."

"Why didn't somebody check?" Her voice sounded shrill even to her own ears. Ryan had pushed her over the edge, and her composure fled. "You know what he's capable of!"

"You have no *idea* what I'm capable of," Ryan said. "And that's your problem. But get used to it, Peyton. There are a lot of people here who won't stand for you being in charge. Not after what I've done to prevent those dirty Scavs from getting in. You make nice with one and I get the job done." Ryan turned on his heel and reached for the door. "We let this one walk, and we're going to pay for it. You might trust that girl, but this one isn't like her. He's not going to turn so easily just because you bat your eyelashes at him. The second you give him some slack, he'll be off. And then there'll be no stopping them."

Peyton let him leave, and as soon as the door clicked shut she rounded on Graham. "How could you have let him?"

"I didn't know. He kept a guard on the door."

She snorted. "Like that would keep you out."

"Sometimes you need to pick and choose your battles, Peyton. What would I have done before you got back? I'm not in charge. *You* are. I'd have been overstepping my bounds."

"Someone needs to stand up for them. Dad would have. I thought you would have, too."

"Before you left you weren't all too concerned with their well-being. What changed out there?"

Peyton crossed her arms over her chest and looked around the dim room. It was hard to believe that just a month ago Nixie had been the one on the hard floor glaring up at her with hatred. And last night they'd slept side by side, curled up around each other. "I woke up," she said simply. "Fighting like this...being two separate people...it's not working, Graham. I'm tired of it. If we didn't fight, Dad wouldn't have died. He'd still be here."

"You wouldn't have met Nixie."

"No, but maybe I wouldn't have had to meet her. Maybe I would have known her all along. Things would be easier. For us. For everyone."

Graham sat down in a folding chair that had been placed near the center of the room facing Ranger. "Tell me what happened."

And she did. Peyton told him everything, from the moment they left, to Static's burn, and Nixie's ability to find water. She told him about the city, getting lost, and Nixie unexpectedly calling up the storm. When she finished, Graham stared at her in disbelief.

"I know! It sounds crazy, and believe me, if I hadn't been there, I wouldn't have believed it myself. But it's all true."

"And the others, do they know about her?"

"No. I figured it out and got her to admit it to me. I didn't tell them. It's her business to tell people, not mine. Please don't say a word."

"Of course I won't. It's just hard to believe. With that kind of ability, she could solve everyone's problems. The crops would flourish."

"I know."

"When it started to rain everyone ran around, trying to collect as much water as possible. It started so suddenly. Do you think she could do it again?"

Peyton nodded. Nixie could do it again if she tried. She believed in her.

"We have to get out of here," Ranger said softly from the bed he lay on.

Nixie leaned over him and gently pressed a cool washcloth over his face to soak off the blood. Jasper stood off to the side near the foot of the bed with his back to them, watching the door. Nixie knew the young guard was listening, or at least trying to, but at least he afforded them the semblance of privacy, and for that, a surge of gratitude rose within her.

"If you're suggesting sneaking out, there's no need. We can leave when you can walk on your own."

He snorted softly in disbelief. "They really have you thinking that?"

"Of course, because it's true."

"Oh, Nixie. I didn't think you were a fool, but they put some crazy ideas in your head."

A flash of annoyance filled her, and she struggled to fight it back. *Ranger is not the enemy. He's a friend, and he means nothing by it. He just doesn't understand.* "The only crazy idea they put there is that we don't have to starve to death. I went out with them. On a mission."

"Why would you help them? They kept you hostage. Or did you forget that?"

She couldn't deny that it had started off that way, but how could she convince him it wasn't like that anymore? She sighed and glanced around. She'd have to show him. "Jasper?" The guard turned. "Can you give us a minute?"

He hesitated, his eyes taking in Ranger's battered body before he gave a short nod and left the room. When Nixie turned back to Ranger, he looked surprised. Or at least as surprised as he could look with the condition he was in.

"Like I said, we can leave when you want. They're not going to keep us here. Most of them are not like Ryan. He's terrible. But the rest are just like us. They're just trying to survive. Only they're doing a better job of it than we are." She dipped the cloth in a basin of water, rinsed it out, and pressed it to his face again. "I want to talk to everyone. Get them to come here for help."

"Faulkner won't like that."

"Faulkner is wrong. About everything. Things could be so much easier. Maybe not like Before, but at least easier than they are now."

Ranger pressed his lips into a thin line despite the split. "We're all alive because of Faulkner. Do you know what you're saying?"

"I know. But remember what I said? About him being touched with the madness?"

He grunted in agreement.

"You said you'd take care of it if he was."

"Keeping us from the Settlers…it was for our own good." Ranger struggled to get the words out. Nixie could hear it in the strain of his voice and the way the one eye couldn't seem to focus on one particular spot. "Since you've been gone, he's been saying weird things. About sins. I don't know what it means."

Nixie changed the subject since the conversation seemed too painful for him. They could talk about it later. "Look, you've only dealt with Ryan. Trust me. If you meet the others, you'll see what I mean. They've been so kind to me. Dr. Easton fixed me up, Avery gave me clothing, and Graham took me in. They could have kept me down in that prison, but they didn't."

"Maybe they just wanted you to be lulled into a false sense of security. So you'd believe them."

"I thought that at first, too. But don't be so cynical, Ranger. Why would they do that? I'm an extra mouth to feed. What do they have to gain? An extra pair of hands? I'm not exactly the strongest person."

"Your abilities."

Nixie shook her head. "They didn't know about that."

"Didn't? You mean they do now?"

"No. Only Peyton."

"Peyton, is she the guard?"

"Yes."

"You seem comfortable with her."

Nixie felt the color rise in her cheeks and couldn't stop it. Comfort didn't quite describe it. Before she could say anything, Ranger started to speak again.

"Nixie, about Faulkner. There's something I need to tell you." When she didn't respond, he took as deep a breath as his injuries would allow. "I should have seen it before, but he's—"

The door burst open and Dr. Easton strode in with Jasper at her heels. In her hands she clutched a bag, which she immediately dumped on the ground. "If I hadn't taken an oath, I'd kill him myself," she swore and brushed Nixie aside.

Nixie moved out of the way as quickly as she could and stood by Jasper at the foot of the bed, alternately amused with the Doctor's entrance and worried about Ranger's reaction to her. When she reached out and touched his face, he jerked back, nearly dislodging himself from the bed.

"Settle down, son. I'm just checking you over. I'm a doctor."

Ranger looked to Nixie for approval, and she smiled. "You're in good hands now."

"But I need to—"

Dr. Easton didn't let him finish. "Not that Nixie didn't do a good job of cleaning you up, but let's get the rest of this fixed and then you need some decent rest and a good meal. If you two wouldn't mind?"

"I'll be back later," Nixie promised as she and Jasper slipped from the room. Ranger started to protest, but once the door clicked shut, virtually all sound died.

"We should probably get some rest," Jasper suggested. Nixie agreed. After the last few days, all she wanted was a comfortable bed for a few hours, because who knew what would happen tomorrow once Ranger was back on his feet. His cut-off words echoed in her ears. What had he been trying to tell her about Faulkner?

CHAPTER THIRTY-ONE

Even though she didn't think she'd sleep soundly due to recent events, Peyton fell into a deep sleep the second her head hit her pillow. She didn't wake up again until early the next morning, with a parched mouth.

After talking to Graham yesterday, she'd decided today she was going to ask Nixie to dance again, to see if she could bring another storm. She believed in her and knew she could do it. And hopefully Nixie believed in herself as well. She had just taken her first sip of fresh, cool water when a light knock sounded on her door. Hoping it wasn't an emergency, she cautiously opened the door, relieved to see Nixie standing on the other side.

"Hi," she said softly, gesturing for her to come in. Nixie returned her smile with one that lit up the darkest places in Peyton's heart, and the muscle beat unevenly twice before righting itself. "Do you want something to drink?" she offered, motioning to her glass.

Nixie shook her head and looked around the room. "You have a lot of things here."

"They belonged to my dad, mostly. He collected things whenever he went out."

Peyton finished her glass of water and set it on the counter, watching Nixie as she moved from shelf to shelf, looking at all the little treasures he'd picked up. Most of them were faded and dirty, and Peyton saw them from someone else's eyes for the first time. She frowned. "He liked to tell stories about them. I remember when I was little, he'd bring something back and tell me some elaborate tale about the person who owned it." She chuckled. "I guess it sounds silly, but I liked listening to him."

"Has it gotten easier?"

"Since he died?" Nixie nodded and Peyton cocked her head, looking up at the ceiling—the only untouched space in the room. "I guess. I don't feel as angry anymore. I still want to catch the people who killed him, but it's not the only thing on my mind anymore. I have other responsibilities. I don't think Dad would want me to spend all of my time out for revenge. He'd want me to be happy."

"Are you?"

Was she? She thought back to the last few weeks. Sure, there were moments of utter loneliness and frustration. Times when she put her job above herself. But more recently there was a pixie-like girl who'd invaded her thoughts and made herself quite at home there. She smiled. "Yeah, I guess I am."

"Why didn't you tell me Ranger came before? I thought they had abandoned me."

She should have known this would come up. Peyton reached up and brushed the mess of her hair off her forehead. "It was right after Dr. Easton let you out. I didn't know you then. We didn't trust each other. I'm sorry. I should have told you after, but by then…I don't know, it just didn't come up."

Nixie glanced back at her and then looked away quickly. She fidgeted, much as Static would when he was nervous, but Peyton dismissed it. Instead she closed the distance between the two of them and pulled Nixie into her arms. "I'm sorry. I really am."

"Do you trust me now?"

"Yes," Peyton nodded quickly. "Yes, of course I do. After everything you've done for us, how could I not?"

They both sighed simultaneously and then broke into a nervous, awkward laugh. Nixie was just short enough that Peyton could rest her chin comfortably on her head. She wrapped her arms around her, holding onto the warmth, and when she breathed in, she could smell the faint, clean scent of freshly fallen rain.

Nixie broke the hold to reach up and kiss her. It was slow and sweet, just like Nixie. She wanted to stay like this, holding her close and kissing her for days, but now that they had that secret out of the way they had some things to discuss.

When Peyton broke the kiss, Nixie looked up at her, disappointment written in her frown. Peyton kissed her quickly once to smooth it away. "I want you to move in with me," she said. When Nixie pulled back, clearly confused, she tried again. "Wow, that came out fast. I do mean it, but I didn't mean to say it like that. What I meant was, I'd like it if you moved in here. I have an extra bedroom, too, and I'm sure living with Graham is nice and all, because he's a great guy, but he's probably a little boring. Maybe?"

Nixie laughed, and the high and bright sound filled Peyton with a sense of peace. Even if the laughter was aimed at her. "I like having my own space for once, but it does get lonely. I don't like to be alone all the time." She paused, biting her lip, then gazed up at Peyton from beneath her lashes. "Would I...have to sleep in another room?"

"No," Peyton blurted, eyes widening. "No, you can sleep wherever you want. My bed is fine. Just fine. What I mean is, I'd like you in my bed." *What the hell is wrong with me?* She cringed and turned away to give her face a moment to cool as Nixie continued to laugh.

"I understand," Nixie finally said as her laughter died down. "I know what you mean. You don't have to be embarrassed."

"Well, I suppose it's good one of us understands. Since my mouth isn't cooperating."

"I think your mouth is cooperating just fine," Nixie replied and pulled Peyton back for another fiery kiss. Peyton had just enough time to respond and wrap her arms around Nixie again when another knock sounded at the door. She groaned and pulled back. "It's going to be one of those days."

Graham stood on the other side of the door, smiling. "Good morning, Peyton. Morning, Nixie. I didn't see you get up and leave. Did you rest well?"

"I don't think I've ever slept deeper," Nixie admitted, taking a seat on a chair as Graham took one opposite her. "Before I came here I tried to see Ranger, but Dr. Easton wouldn't let me in. She said it was too early."

"Good old Doc. She's very strict when it comes to her patients. You'll be able to see him later."

"I wonder how he's taking to bed rest. Ranger has never been able to stay still for very long."

Graham chuckled. "Well, even if he's throwing a fit, she won't let him get out of bed. She'll strap him down and sedate him if he needs it. Anyway, I must be honest, I didn't come here for just a casual chat, I'm afraid, as nice as it is. There's something I'm curious about."

Peyton looked to Graham and Nixie caught the movement between them because she seemed to deflate on her chair just a bit. "Oh?" Her voice came out thin and softer than ever.

"You're not in trouble, if that's what you're thinking," Graham said. "But Peyton did tell me something that I found rather interesting, and I wanted to talk to you about it."

Nixie spun to look at her, her eyes wide. "You swore you wouldn't tell," she cried.

"But it's Graham. He's not going to hurt you or make you do anything you don't want," she said, trying to reassure her. Carefully she placed her hand on Nixie's knee, hoping the touch would anchor her and keep her from running out the door.

"No, I would never make you do anything. I was hoping you would show me because your gift could help everyone, but I understand if you don't want to."

"Do you trust us?" Peyton asked, leaning close. Her hand never left its spot on Nixie's knee.

Nixie stared at the warm, affectionate hand on her leg and then looked at Graham and Peyton in turn. Did she trust them? Even with Peyton not telling her about Ranger? After everything that had happened, yes, of course she did. And it wasn't like she wasn't keeping her own secret. *Don't think about it.* But could she trust herself not to screw it up?

"What if I can't do it?" she asked softly, more for herself than the others.

"I believe in you. I know you can do it," Peyton said.

Graham added, "Then you can't do it, and that's okay."

But it's not okay. I want to help everyone. "I'll try."

"When?" Peyton asked eagerly. "I mean, it's your call."

If Ranger wanted to leave when he was feeling well, then the sooner she did this, the better. "Now?" she asked.

❖

Nixie hadn't been on the roof of the building, and she could see why. There were a few raised beds scattered here and there, but most of the roof was covered in solar panels angled toward the sun. Only a few open spaces remained, and Nixie wondered how she'd be able to work.

Walking to the center of the area, she surveyed the space and then turned back to Peyton and Graham. They stood just a little beyond the access door and nodded to her encouragingly.

Nixie hadn't been aware of what she was doing yesterday—had it really been only a day? So she closed her eyes and tried to recall the feeling. The cleansing scent of rain washed over her. Again it was just outside of her reach, calling to her, tantalizing her, but this time she reached out for it. She tried to pull the scent closer to her and wrap it around her, welcoming it with outstretched arms. Taking two tentative steps forward, the scent grew stronger. Another step and it was almost there. She tried once more and barked her shin on one of the solar panels.

Biting back a groan she opened her eyes. The scent started to bleed away, so she adjusted her position on the roof and tried again. Arms up and open, pulling the pleasing odor back to her, trying to make it into a blanket she could wrap around her body.

Her feet moved of their own accord as she stepped carefully across the roof. This time she met with no obstacles, and she fell into a rhythm. The pulse of the rain just beyond her reach became a tempo she could dance to, and her body ached to feel it beat time against her skin. The wind picked up and lifted her hair from her shoulders as she stepped and twirled faster. The first drops of rain splattered against her skin, soaking into her clothing and quenching her almost permanent thirst. She soaked it up like sand in the desert and called the rain to her faster.

Behind her she heard murmurs but could not make out the words. Peyton and Graham talking. This time she kept her surroundings in focus as much as she could. The first time she didn't know what she was doing, but this time she could feel their presence behind her, offering wordless encouragement. She smiled as she danced. When she stepped faster, the rain fell heavily. When she slowed her pace, the rain eased to a gentle sprinkle that caressed the plants and her body as it fell to the earth.

A sudden commotion behind her disrupted her concentration and she stopped her dance abruptly. Around her the rain continued to fall gently as she turned to face Graham and Peyton, only to find them confronting Ryan.

"What the hell is this?" he yelled, his voice a discordant note unsettling the peaceful hum of the rain. He looked between Nixie and the rain, at her still outstretched arms and stared in wonder.

"Ryan, just go back inside. This doesn't concern you." Peyton's words broke his trance.

He shook off his surprise and his eyes narrowed as his lips curled up in disgust. "The Travelers talked about freaks like you, but I never thought the stories were true."

"Go back inside," Graham urged, blocking Ryan's advance.

"You knew about this? You knew she could do this? Why did you wait so long to make her? Our crops are *dying*," he said, his voice a shrill scream as he forced his way past his two fellow Settlers. He stood between them, looking back and forth. "Why would you coddle her and make her life comfortable, when she's caused you nothing but grief, Peyton? Are you that blind? That you let a pretty face get in the way of your common sense? Not much of a leader, are you?"

"What are you talking about?" Peyton spat, taking a step toward Ryan. Graham held on to her arm, barely restraining her, but she ceased her movements.

"What am I talking about? Ha! You're nothing but a joke. Some great leader you've turned out to be. What a way to honor your father by falling for the bitch who killed him."

Nixie took a step back, gasping, mimicking Graham and Peyton.

"How *dare* you," Peyton started, but the rest of her words failed her.

Graham stepped in, calm as ever even as Nixie's world started crumbling around her. "That's a large accusation, Ryan. You know we don't accuse people here without evidence."

"Evidence? I'd say a confession counts. That dirty Scav's friend admitted everything. He killed Enrique and she stood there and watched. Bet she didn't tell you that, did she?" Ryan turned to face Nixie, his face marred by a sneer. "You Scavs try to act so tough, but you talk pretty easily. You were there the night Enrique was killed."

He turned back to Peyton. "You wanted revenge, didn't you? Well now we have him, and it's all thanks to me."

He continued to speak, but Nixie didn't hear his words. She looked past him, trying desperately to catch Peyton's eyes, but the girl wouldn't look up at her. She looked just beyond her, as if she didn't exist, and Nixie's heart started falling to pieces as the rain subsided.

"Peyton, please," she whispered.

"You were there," Peyton finally said once Ryan had stopped talking. "You were there, and you watched my father die, and this whole time you've been telling me you didn't know what happened. You *lied* to me."

"You lied to me, too," Nixie said weakly, but it was useless. A small part of Nixie wanted to continue the lie to preserve herself, but she couldn't. Not anymore. What good would it do when the truth would just come out in the end and make things even worse? She hung her head, frustrated for not being honest in the first place. *But I didn't know her then. I hated her for what she was.*

"All you Scavs are alike—dirty, thieving murderers." Ryan's words went straight through her and she jerked her head up to look at him. The smug look on his face tore apart the last shreds of her composure and it snapped like a taut wire.

Nixie launched herself at Ryan, her fists out. He dodged her first blow, but she caught him on the second. She might have been small, but she was faster than he expected. He stopped her before she could get a second blow in.

"Peyton, where are you going?"

Nixie spun at the sound of Graham's voice, just in time to see her disappear into the access door. She wrenched herself free from Ryan's grasp and chased after her, calling out as she went.

CHAPTER THIRTY-TWO

Where is he?" Peyton yelled as she burst through Dr. Easton's door. The rage that had held her in its grip after Dad died bubbled to the surface and threatened to boil over. His murderer was in their home taking advantage of their kindness and using their supplies. On the way down from the roof she thought she heard Dad's voice calling out to her, begging her to be reasonable and think everything through, but she refused to listen.

Not even his ghost would make her change her mind.

Ryan was right. She hated to admit it, but he was. Everyone had been laughing behind her back. Especially Nixie. The name stabbed through her chest and she struggled to suck in a breath. She'd deal with the devastation of her betrayal later, but for now, she had bigger fish to fry.

"What's the meaning of this?" Dr. Easton appeared through one of the doorways, frowning. "You can't just come slamming through the door like that, Peyton. I have patients resting."

"Like hell you do. Where is the Scavenger? He's not staying with us any longer."

"Excuse me?"

"He killed Dad. He admitted it to Ryan."

"Since when do you listen to Ryan?"

"Since Nixie pretty much confirmed it. Where is he?"

Dr. Easton backed up and barred one of the doors. "Why do you want to see him? I don't think I should let you in when you're clearly in distress."

"Get out of my way."

"I refuse. When it comes to my patients, I pull rank over you. If you don't leave now, I'll have you removed. Don't make this difficult, Peyton. I know you're still grieving, but you will not harm this man. Not while he's under my care."

Peyton advanced and stood toe-to-toe with the older woman. She didn't want to involve her, but if she wouldn't move, she had no choice. "Then release him from your care."

"You would go after a man who can't defend himself?"

"He went after my father and the others, and they were unarmed."

"Two wrongs don't make a right, Peyton."

"No, but it'll make me feel a hell of a lot better."

Dr. Easton sighed. "Maybe for a little while, but I know the pain you're feeling. It will fester like an infected wound and just get worse. Killing him will not bring your father back, and it won't make what he did right." A commotion at the door distracted Dr. Easton long enough for Peyton to push past her into the room. Ranger lay on the bed, his eyes half-lidded and looking up at her as best he could. It was only when she saw him lying there that she realized she hadn't brought anything with her to take care of the problem. She glanced around the room.

"I'm sorry about your father," he managed before her hands closed around his throat.

"Don't you *dare* speak about him when you killed him!" she cried. He closed his eyes and gasped as her hands closed tighter. The more she thought about it, the hotter her fury burned, and the more her hands gripped.

There was a sound behind her, a blur, and a sharp pain in her shoulder as she was knocked off balance. Her grip loosened for only a moment, but it was enough, because suddenly Nixie was between her and Ranger.

"Get out of my way."

"No!" Nixie cried, the look in her eyes wild. "I know you're angry, Peyton, but you can't kill him! We were just doing what we had to in order to survive."

"You attacked them and then killed him. How is that surviving?"

"We were desperate. You don't understand what it's like to live the way we do. You have everything provided for you."

"We *work* for what we have. It doesn't just fall from the sky."

"It's still easier. You have technology we could only dream of."

"You lied to me, Nixie. You told me you didn't know who killed him, and you were right there when it happened."

"I'm sorry. I know it's not enough, and I know I shouldn't have lied to you, but I didn't know you like I do now, and I was scared. You would have killed me."

Peyton opened her mouth to deny it, but she couldn't. She would have killed her. She was so bent on revenge that she wouldn't have hesitated. Like she hadn't hesitated to come after Ranger moments ago. The realization slammed into her with painful accuracy and she cringed. *I'm a monster.* She took a step back, her gaze moving between Ranger and Nixie. She put even more space between them. "Dr. Easton." She called to the woman in the doorway and beckoned her forward without taking her eyes from Nixie.

"Are you done?"

She couldn't answer that question. Couldn't admit to what she'd nearly done. "Don't let them leave. I want them to remain here."

"For how long?"

"Until I tell you otherwise." She stepped from the room and Dr. Easton followed her, shutting the door behind her.

"I'm not going to make my hospital into a prison just because you're angry."

"I didn't ask you to. Just hold them for now. I don't want them wandering around."

"May I ask what you intend to do with them?" Dr. Easton asked as she reached the door exiting the hospital wing.

Peyton didn't like the tone of her voice, but she couldn't blame her. She rested her hand on the handle. "I don't know yet."

"Are you all right?" Nixie asked as soon as Peyton had left the room and they were alone. She checked Ranger's neck, noting the imprints of Peyton's fingers that were already starting to bruise.

"I'll live. Thanks to you."

"She would have stopped."

"No, Nixie. She wouldn't have. She was going to kill me with her bare hands, or did you miss the part where her hands were around my throat?" The talking aggravated him and he started to cough, so Nixie got up and found him a glass of water. "Thanks," he said hoarsely after he had taken a sip.

"I've never seen her like that."

"You've only known her a month."

"But she isn't like that," Nixie protested. "She would never have—"

"Grief makes people do things they normally wouldn't."

"Why did you tell Ryan?"

Ranger turned away from her and looked at the distant wall. "There's only so much torture a person can take until they crack." He sighed and closed his eyes. Nixie rested a hand on his shoulder. "I thought I was stronger, but I guess I have lower limits than I thought."

"Cracking doesn't mean you aren't strong."

"Faulkner would say otherwise. At least I didn't tell him where the camp is. Funny, he stopped as soon as I admitted I'd killed that guard."

"Ryan and Peyton hate each other. I'm sure that information was just as good to him as anything else. Better, because he could shove it in her face."

The door opened and Nixie looked back to see Dr. Easton enter. She shook her head sadly and approached them, her hands in the pockets of her lab coat.

"Seems I'm supposed to keep the two of you here for the time being," she said, sitting down on a chair at the foot of the bed.

"And then what?" Nixie asked.

"I don't know. But Peyton won't kill you. I made sure of that. I think she would have snapped out of it before she actually did it anyway. I'm sorry I didn't stop her before she got to you, Ranger."

"It happens," he said, trying for a light tone and failing.

"Not on my watch, it doesn't."

Ranger shrugged. "I've been through worse, believe me."

"I'm sure you have. But this is a place for rest and healing. Not attempted murder." She groaned as she pushed herself back out of the chair. "I'm getting too old for this. I'll make up the other bed for you, Nixie. You can share this room with Ranger."

"Thank you. Can I do anything to help?"

"I appreciate the offer, but no. Aside from watching over him, that is."

Nixie nodded. "Of course."

"I'm sure Peyton will send someone down to guard the entrance. At least it won't be Ryan. If she has any common sense in her head, at least." She glanced over her shoulder at them. "Get comfortable. Who knows how long you'll be here."

CHAPTER THIRTY-THREE

The crash echoed throughout the apartment and Peyton stared at the disaster before her. She'd upended one of the tables, scattering the contents across the room. What had she done? What had she almost done? She held out her trembling hands before her and stared at them. She could still see Ranger's throat between them, his eyes widening as he struggled to suck in a breath.

"What have I done?" she asked, hoping someone would answer her.

You didn't kill him. You stopped yourself before you did. The voice sounded like her father, and she choked out a sob.

No! Nixie stopped me before I went too far. I would have killed him if she hadn't been there. "I wish you were here, Dad. I can't do this without you." The silence in response to her words was unbearable. Her chest ached and she struggled to breathe. When she managed to suck in air, it burned her lungs. Hot tears rolled down her face, which she buried in her hands.

What was she doing? This was crazy. All of it. Visions of her hands around a tanned throat blurred everything else out. She wasn't a leader. How could she lead when she couldn't even control her own emotions? Dad never lost control. She'd never be like him. The strident scream that pushed past her lips echoed around the vast, empty room, and it was a wonder no one knocked on the door to check on her.

But they probably already know what I've done.
No one will want to be around me again.

Decisions had to be made. She couldn't keep Ranger and Nixie locked away forever. She couldn't kill them. In the last few weeks—most of it over the course of the last three days—Nixie had grown on her to a degree she hadn't thought possible. An innocuous, four-letter word loomed menacingly before her, taunting her, but she pushed it out of her mind. There was no way. No way she'd fallen in...love...with Nixie. But even if it were true, she couldn't trust herself anymore. She had to let them go. Exhaustion crept over her body and she pushed feebly to her feet, only to collapse on the worn couch. A patchwork quilt Dad had given her one year lay across the back, and she pulled it down onto her body and wrapped it around herself. Moments later, the comforting warmth had seeped into her as her sobs quieted. Closing her eyes, she tried to quiet her mind, but as she drifted into a restless sleep, a vision of Ranger, dead, swam before her.

❖

A quiet knock on the door frame alerted Nixie to a visitor, and she glanced up from her watch over Ranger to see Jasper standing there uneasily.

"Hey," he said. He looked over his shoulder and entered, and then shut the door behind him. "So, Dr. Easton told me what happened."

"Did Peyton send you?"

"Nope. Can't say she did. Just wandered down here on my own. Wanted to get a better look at your friend." He offered her a large grin. "I'm nosy."

Nixie couldn't help the smile as her fears faded. "He's sleeping."

Jasper strolled over, his hands hooked in his back pockets. He looked down on Ranger and cringed. "She did a number on him."

"Why aren't you angry? Don't you know why she did it?"

"I do." He circled around the bed and propped himself up on the edge of the counter. "And I'm processing it. But for some reason, I'm having a hard time getting upset about it."

"Why?"

"I can't explain it. I mean, don't get me wrong, I'm upset Enrique died. And it wasn't like it was that long ago. But I don't know, maybe…maybe I'm going soft. Maybe you changed my mind about things. Everything happens for a reason, right?"

Did everything happen for a reason? Nixie fidgeted in her chair while Jasper leaned against the counter as if he hadn't a care in the world. And maybe he didn't. Nixie hadn't known him all that long.

He broke into her thoughts as he pushed off the counter and paced back to the door. "Anyway, I didn't mean to interrupt anything. I just wanted to check on the two of you and all that. I'm sure you're exhausted. I know I am." As if on cue, Nixie yawned, which set Jasper off. "Aargh! I hate that," he said once he'd finished. "They're so contagious."

Nixie chuckled and Ranger shifted in his sleep. With that, Jasper held a finger up to his lips, winked, and let himself out. The weight of the day crashed onto her shoulders as the door shut behind him, and she looked at the bed Dr. Easton had set up for her. She kicked off her shoes and, after a last check on Ranger, stumbled over and climbed between the sheets. Immediately her eyelids drooped and she yawned violently. The mattress was wonderfully soft after sleeping on the hard ground, and though the temperature of the room was perfect, the blankets over her added another layer of warmth and coziness.

As sleep clouded her mind, she realized it was a feeling she might be missing soon. It might be the last night she spent at the Mill, and the prospect of returning to her camp sat like a rock in her stomach. A month ago she would have done anything to get out. Even a week ago, she would have happily walked out the door. She'd been ready to return to her people, even if only to convince them to join a settlement. But now? Even with Peyton turning on her and Ranger, she didn't want to leave. Even if Peyton hated her, she'd miss the companionship of teasing Jasper and twitchy Static. She'd miss the warmth of Graham and his kind smile, and Avery's generosity. She wanted to be at the Mill when Avery's baby was born so she could coo over it and learn what name they had decided on for the child.

If she had to leave, she'd miss all those things, and she wasn't ready for that.

Please don't let this be the end.

CHAPTER THIRTY-FOUR

Have a seat," Graham said, gesturing to one of the chairs around his table. He slid a steaming mug of tea toward Peyton as she took the offered chair.

Silence descended over them as she sipped the amber liquid. She trained her eyes just inside the rim of the mug to keep from meeting Graham's gaze.

"Have you made a decision?" he finally asked after giving her time. His fingers drummed lightly on the scarred surface of the table, creating a light staccato rhythm.

"There's really only one possible outcome," she murmured.

"Is there? I can think of quite a few. Killing them, for one. You seemed hell-bent on doing that yesterday," he said, his voice taking on a hard edge that she'd never heard from him before.

"No, not that. I was angry yesterday."

"So you lashed out and nearly choked a man to death. An injured man who couldn't defend himself. Seems logical to me."

Peyton threw her hands in the air, letting out a frustrated growl. "I can't help that I lost my mind for a moment."

"Dangerous thing to have happen. After that display I'm starting to wonder whether or not Ryan would have been the better choice."

Silence settled over them, thick and heavy, as Peyton stared in astonishment. Graham didn't turn away and hardly blinked as he stared at her. The lines around his eyes were drawn tight, and the edges of his lips curled down in a frown. He seemed older than ever in that moment, and Peyton hung her head in shame. "I'm sorry," she whispered. "I know it's not enough, but I am sorry. I lost control of myself and I shouldn't have. But when I saw him, and knew he'd killed Dad…Did you know?"

"No, I didn't. Ryan kept that gem in his pocket."

"Aren't you angry?"

"Of course! But that doesn't mean I'm going to kill him."

Peyton pushed back from the table, knocking into it and nearly upsetting her cup of tea. "But there needs to be justice. Dad deserves that. And there's no system in place like Before."

"No, but I've never thought that was a bad thing. You don't know what it was like, Peyton. Men did something wrong, went to prison, and came out hard. It changed them, and not in a good way. And more often than not they ended up right back where they started with longer sentences. I'm not saying what we have now is perfect, but I wouldn't want to go back to that."

Peyton began to pace across the room. Graham turned and followed her movements. She ran her hands through her hair a few times, tugging at the ends much like she saw Static do when he was frustrated.

"So what are you going to do?"

"Let them go."

At that his eyes widened. "Both of them? Nixie, too?"

"It's the only way. She lied to me. I can't let her stay here. I'll banish them."

"Maybe I misread something, but it seemed to me like the two of you had grown much closer on that mission. And you're willing to simply throw that away?"

Peyton barked out a harsh laugh that tore at her throat. "It's hard to keep the same opinion of someone after they lie to you. Especially when it concerns your father's murder. Everything I know about her is built on a lie. How can I trust her after this?"

"I'm not condoning what she did or said. But think about the situation. She didn't know you then, and when she was here, it wasn't exactly under her volition."

Though it ripped at her heart to say it, she said, "I can't. She needs to leave. This is Dad we're talking about. I don't understand how you don't feel the same way. I thought you loved him, too." She turned to the door, not bothering to finish her tea.

"Peyton, wait," he called, and she turned back to face him. "I loved your father, but his death taught me not to take things for granted. You only get one chance in this life. Don't throw it away because of a misunderstanding."

She nodded, said good-bye, and left. Graham didn't understand the war raging through her. If she let Nixie stay, every time she looked at her she'd see more than those cool blue eyes and beautiful smile. She'd see her father's dead body lying on Dr. Easton's table, waiting to be dressed for his burial.

The sooner she got this over with, the faster she could move on.

❖

"I don't know about you, but all this sitting around is making me nervous," Ranger said. He'd finally managed to sit up on his own and eat, but now the inactivity was getting to him. "I don't like it. I need to be doing something."

"That's because you never rest," Nixie teased as she paced the floor.

"I wish they'd at least let us outside," he added with a sigh as he glanced at the window wistfully. "This whole being cooped up I don't like."

"It's because you're not used to it."

"And you are? Look at you. Just a month here and you're already a full-fledged Settler."

She tossed a glare in his direction.

"No, but really. I worry she'll come back and decide to finish what she started. Normally, I could take her, but my ribs." He looked down at the bandaging and winced after he prodded it gently.

"You're lucky they're just bruised."

"Then what's a bandage going to do?"

Nixie shrugged. "I'm not the doctor. Ask her."

"Ask me what?" Dr. Easton said as she entered the room. She carried a small bottle in one hand and a glass of water in the other. "This is for your pain," she said as she handed it to Ranger. He didn't hesitate as he tossed it back.

And he thinks I've made myself right at home. He's been here less time than I have. Certainly took to the doctor faster than I did.

"Have you heard anything from Peyton?" Nixie asked cautiously. Dr. Easton just shook her head and placed the glass on the counter.

"Can't say I have, sorry. But I'm sure you'll hear from her today. Eventually."

She left without another word and they waited for the door to shut, but a commotion outside drew Nixie to the door.

Julian supported Avery as he led the way. Her face contorted in a rictus of pain on one step and she doubled over.

"Avery!" Julian said, worry in his tone.

"I'm fine. It's just a contraction."

Nixie hurried toward her, grasping her arm. "You're in labor?" She didn't give her a chance to answer before she was rushing on. "How are you feeling? Is the pain bad? Did your water break? That's silly, of course it broke. Do you want me to leave? Dr. Easton!"

Avery laughed as the older woman came into the room, shaking her head. "I know she's here, Nixie. Calm down and give the woman some space."

Nixie immediately stepped back and let Avery and Julian enter. She tried to give her space but followed close behind. "Is there anything I can do to help?"

"No, nothing right now. Thank you. Just go back to keep—"

Screams from the front of the building interrupted her and they all froze and turned toward the door. Nixie spun around, watching the door, waiting for someone to burst in.

"What was that?" Ranger asked after a moment, breaking the silence.

"I don't know."

"I should go check." Julian hesitated. He glanced at Avery and she pulled him down for a kiss.

"Go. It's your job."

As Julian opened the door to leave, the sounds of screaming filtered into the room and Nixie tossed a nervous glance at Dr. Easton. She ushered Avery into another room and called back over her shoulder, "I know Peyton wants you to stay here, but maybe you should go check that out. Let me know what's going on."

"Right." Nixie popped her head into Ranger's room. "I'll be back. Stay here."

"Not going very far."

People were running up and down the hallway in confusion, with shouts of *What's happening?* and *It's at the front!* filling the air. Nixie got swept into the crush of bodies and she latched onto Cooper as he passed.

"What's going on?"

"Someone said there's a fire at the front of the building. I don't know. I thought you were supposed to be with Dr. Easton."

"She sent me to check it out. She's with Avery."

"Great time for Avery to pop. If it's a fire, and we don't get it put out fast, we're screwed."

Cooper used his body to push through the crowd, shouting for them to move out of the way. Nixie pressed against his back, afraid of being separated. They didn't make it far before another person screamed behind them.

"It's Scavengers! They're throwing fire!"

"What?" Nixie whipped around. An apartment door opened, and smoke poured through. "Cooper! There's a fire in here!"

He followed her into the apartment, where the smoke overwhelmed them. Glass from the window lay shattered on the ground, and the carpet was up in flames.

"How could they do this?" Cooper asked, staring at the flames as they ate the carpet and crawled toward the hardwood floor. Sparks leapt onto the plastic blinds and they twisted and curled as they melted.

Another crash startled them as a bottle hurtled through the window and erupted into more flames. They jumped back in horror as the upholstered furniture caught. "We need water! Quick!" she screamed as they both dashed for the kitchen.

It wouldn't be enough. They needed help, she realized, as the water took its time coming out of the faucet. Cooper carried the first pot of water to the furniture and dumped the contents over the flames, but it hardly mattered.

"We need more." She left the second pot filling and ran for the door, screaming for help and water. The doors across the hall opened, and soon a flood of people had formed a line, helping move loaded pots and pans to the apartment that had turned into an inferno.

The fire spread up the walls despite the brick because of the pictures taped there. One of the men got too close to the flames and burned his arm.

"Nixie, go tell Dr. Easton what's happening."

"But I have to help here," she argued.

"Just go! She needs to be prepared for injuries."

God, she can't deal with that right now. Not with Avery in labor. She nodded and sprinted for the door.

The medical wing was quiet compared to the front of the building, and Nixie burst into the room. She heard a scream from the back and cringed but followed the sound. Avery lay back in a bed, sweat covering her face. She glanced at Nixie as she appeared in the doorway and she smiled wanly.

"Dr. Easton," Nixie said, not wanting to distract her.

"What's happening out there?" she asked. She never took her eyes from Avery.

"There're fires breaking out. It's…it's the Scavengers."

That got the doctor's attention. She glanced quickly at Nixie before turning back to her task.

"They're throwing bottles of fire. I don't know how."

"Sounds like Molotov cocktails. They were used for rioting Before. Where'd he get flammable material is what I'm wondering. Does he make moonshine?"

"Moonshine?" Nixie frowned. "I don't even know what that is."

"It's alcohol. Made from grains. Does he have a car radiator set up anywhere, away from camp?"

Nixie thought back to her visits to his tent and saw all the bottles filled with a clear liquid. She had assumed it was water. Then there were the trips to that field where they'd stolen grain that was never made into bread for the people.

Bread they desperately needed.

"I haven't seen it, but he probably does." She told her about the grain, and Dr. Easton nodded.

"Most likely is, then. Go back and help them. I'm sure they'll need all the help they can get."

"But what about you? If they start coming in with burns—"

"I'll manage. Avery isn't going anywhere anytime soon."

As Nixie left the room, she was greeted by Ranger. He leaned against the doorway of his room, one arm around his ribs. "I'm going with you," he said.

"You should be in bed," she argued, but he brushed off her arm even as he winced.

"I can't just lie around. It's Faulkner out there. I should have known he'd do something like this. I was listening to Dr. Easton, and she's right. He has moonshine. I should have realized what he was doing, but he doesn't tell me everything. Listen to me. He really has gone crazy."

"What? But..." Hadn't he been defending him earlier? No, she realized. He hadn't, not really.

"Moonshine is strong stuff. It's okay when you make it right, but running it through an old radiator? He's been poisoning himself with the stuff, and it's made him crazy."

"He's been drinking the stuff they're throwing at the Mill? The stuff that's setting it on fire?" she asked, incredulous. It was unbelievable that something so flammable could be consumed by a human. But then, it would drive a man crazy to have that liquid in him.

"I didn't realize it. I should have. All those bottles in his tent. I'm an idiot, Nix. A complete idiot."

"Come on, then. Let's go."

The two of them headed for the front of the building where everyone else was. More apartments were on fire, and those on the inside continued passing through pots, pans, and anything that could hold water to help combat the flames, but it wasn't enough. The fire was spreading and ate at some of the floorboards. In one of the rooms it licked at the rafters.

"We need more water!" someone screamed.

Another shouted back, "The water pressure! The water is just dripping out!"

Peyton rounded the corner with Willow and Jasper flanking her and others who looked like guards. She spotted Nixie.

"Nixie! What are you doing?"

"Helping," she said from the line she'd joined. Ranger struggled to hold the pot, and Jasper rushed forward to help him.

Peyton pulled her from the line, holding her shoulders at arm's length. "We're losing water. The river. It stopped flowing. I think they did something to dam it farther upriver and we're running out. We're going to lose the building."

Nixie stared at her in horror. Without water, everything would be lost. All the food they'd stored, all of their technology. "I can help," she said suddenly. "Get me to the roof, and I can help."

Peyton nodded and grabbed her hand, entwining their fingers together. The anger she'd had the night before was gone, replaced with relief. She tugged her along and Willow led them to the side stairs, getting everyone to move as they followed in her wake.

I can do this. I can help them save the building.

CHAPTER THIRTY-FIVE

The upper floors had fewer people on the stairs, and for that Peyton was grateful. She didn't want to hurt anyone in her hurry, but she had to follow Nixie. Seeing her in the line with everyone else, helping to put out the fire, doused the flames of hatred in her heart. Who was she trying to fool? She couldn't make her leave.

"I need to make it rain," Nixie said as they ran onto the roof. Willow had left them on the fourth floor to join the rest downstairs.

"The rain won't be enough. Besides, it won't get into the building to put out the fire."

"No, it won't, but if it rains hard enough, it'll burst the dam they built and give us enough water to combat it. Please, Peyton, just let me try."

Us.

She'd said it would give *us* enough water.

Peyton's chest constricted at the inclusiveness of the word. She nodded, and Nixie ran to the center of the roof. She closed her eyes, turned her back on Peyton, and began her dance.

Once Peyton had watched Nixie start and felt sure she was safe, she ran back into the building and nearly collided with Graham.

"Go help everyone. I'll watch over her," he said.

She threw her arms around him and hugged him tightly. "Thank you. You were right." She didn't elaborate, but she didn't need to.

The main entrance to the building was blocked by fire. Most people were fleeing out the back, and she fought against the waves of people. Some moved out of her way, but most rushed past in sheer blind panic.

"Let me through!" she cried, stumbling as she was jostled around. Time was wasting, and each second counted. She had to get to the door and face the Scavengers and buy some time for Nixie. Turning the corner, she finally reached the door and pushed her way through, realizing too late that the only weapon she had was a short hunting knife clipped onto her belt.

A group of Scavengers stood at the end of the bridge holding an array of makeshift weapons. Most looked to be branches with sharpened tips, though a few held crude bows and arrows. Peyton placed her hand on the handle of her knife and pulled it out of its sheath.

Hopefully none of those arrows can fly.

"Stop this!" she called in a loud, clear voice. "What is it you want?"

An older man stepped forward, his gray hair a knotted wreath around his head. Even from a distance she could see the crazed look in his eyes. "It's time you Settlers pay for the crimes you've committed against Nature."

"Crimes? What crimes?"

"The world fell for the sins of humanity, and you attempt to bring us back to that age with your machines. We cannot let that happen."

"Our technology helps us survive. There is nothing wrong with it. We will share it with you if you stop this."

"You offer it out of desperation." The man turned back to his people. "Don't listen to her. It's a Settler trick. You know what these people are capable of."

"No! Nixie was going to come back to you and make an offer!"

At Nixie's name, the people turned to each other, murmuring words she couldn't hear. The man yelled at them to shut up.

"But Faulkner—" one started.

So this is their leader. He's insane. No wonder Nixie seems to fear him.

"Where is Nixie? You speak of her, and yet I don't see her with you. You stole her from us. How do we know she's even alive? And Ranger. Where is he?"

More murmurs from the Scavengers, and Faulkner grinned.

Peyton started to speak, to protest that she was alive, but the low rumble of thunder drowned her out. Everyone looked to the sky in wonder as clouds moved in with unnatural speed.

Nixie. You did it.

The sky opened up. A torrential downpour soaked Settler and Scavenger alike as it came down with a force Peyton had never seen. Some of the Scavengers lifted their arms to the sky, shouting with laughter. Peyton could understand how they felt; she wanted to laugh with them.

To her left, the flames outside the building sputtered as the rain fell, and to her right a sudden roar caught her attention. She and Faulkner turned simultaneously to see a wave of water barreling down the river.

"How?" He turned to stare at her.

She smirked. "Looks like your dam wasn't very strong, was it?" Water raced under the bridge, carrying debris from the dam with it. As the water filled the lines she heard shouts inside the building that the water was flowing again, and she breathed a sigh of relief. They'd get the fires under control. Thanks to Nixie.

"You bitch," Faulkner snarled. He spun around and grabbed one of the weapons from another Scavenger and turned, taking aim. Peyton stared in disbelief as the weapon produced was not a crudely made bow of wood, but a gleaming, deadly crossbow from Before.

The heavy metal door behind her banged open and a body blurred past her, knocking her to the side. She heard a shout a second later as she slammed into the metal railing.

Ranger staggered back, one arm hanging dead at his side. He turned to look at Peyton in shock, and then collapsed. An arrow stuck out from just below his shoulder. An arrow meant for her.

"You shot Ranger!" one of the Scavengers cried.

The door banged open again and Jasper appeared at her side. He held one of the few pistols the Mill had, and he lifted it to take aim just as Faulkner raised the crossbow again.

Peyton yelled out a warning, reaching for Jasper to push him away. A shot rang out.

Faulkner dropped the crossbow and staggered backward, clutching his chest. He looked down at the wound, and then crumpled. The Scavengers gathered around him as Jasper thrust the pistol into Peyton's hand and dropped to Ranger's side.

"Ranger! Hang in there," he said, turning his face to force the man to look at him.

Ranger looked up, his hand around the arrow shaft and pressing the wound. Jasper covered his hand carefully.

"Don't try to pull it out. We'll get you up to Dr. Easton, and she'll get you fixed right up," Jasper promised, looking up at Peyton. "Get help!"

Peyton spun on her heels and ripped open the metal door just as another shot rang out.

This time from the roof.

Calling the rain came easier this time. Nixie hardly had to think about it before the thunder rolled around her and the sky opened and brought the life-saving rain. The harder and faster she danced, the faster the rain came. She moved in ways she didn't think possible, contorting her body and throwing her arms wide.

At one point she thought she'd tear a muscle with the force in her moves, but she just let herself go deeper into the dance, temporarily losing herself to the storm.

It was the gunshot that pulled her back to the present.

Startled, she turned to look at Graham, who was already racing toward the edge of the roof. She moved in that direction as well and just beat him to it. They both struggled to look over the high sides but couldn't see anything.

"Is Peyton all right," she yelled over the roar of the rain.

"Do your people have guns?"

"No, of course not. Where would we get them?"

Graham murmured something inaudible. "I think this rain will help."

"I hope so. I've never seen it like this."

And she hadn't. The water came down so quickly it was hard to see a foot in front of her. When she turned, she realized she could hardly see the other side of the roof.

"I hope it doesn't drown the crops," she said, though Graham didn't answer her.

Water ran down her face in thick streams, and her clothing molded to her body. Beside her, the older man shivered and she put a hand on his shoulder.

"You should go inside!"

"What about you?"

"Me? I love the rain!" Despite the dangerous situation below, she laughed. She felt free for the first time in her life, and she spun in circles with her arms outstretched. Graham laughed with her. As she neared the center of the roof again, the access door opened. She spun to it with a smile on her face, which was quickly wiped away when Ryan stepped through the open doorway.

"Ryan," Graham said, quickly moving to her side. "What are you doing up here? Shouldn't you be helping Peyton with the Scavengers?"

"I am helping her. With the one up here."

He raised his arms and Nixie was staring at the barrel of a gun. She took a step back.

"Put that down!" Graham yelled, pushing Nixie behind him. "Are you crazy? Nixie's helping us!"

"The only thing she's helping do is brainwash us. She's got Peyton wrapped around her little finger."

"Oh, shut it, Ryan. You've always hated Peyton. Stop pretending you're worried about her now when it suits you."

"It's not her I'm worried about. She's got the Doc wrapped in her web, too. Soon our medical supplies will start disappearing. She'll give everything to those Scavs and then where will we be?" He shook his head slowly from side to side. "You should have picked me, Graham. We wouldn't be in this mess if you'd picked a man for the job."

"What I'm looking at isn't a man but a spoiled little boy."

The first shot rang out and Nixie screamed. Graham's leg started to buckle and she reached forward to help him just as the second and third shots fired. He dropped to the ground before she had a chance to catch him.

"Graham!" she screamed, dropping to her knees and turning him onto his back. But he didn't respond. His eyes stared lifelessly at the sky. "No, oh God, no," she cried, knowing it was too late but trying to shake him awake anyway. "How could you?"

Ryan stopped less than two feet away from her, and she looked up to find the gun leveled at her head. He grinned and his finger twitched on the trigger. Nixie closed her eyes.

I never got to tell Peyton I love her.

Ryan cursed. She cracked one eye open as he pulled the trigger again and then swore. Relief coursed through her body as realization dawned: he was out of bullets.

Graham had saved her life.

The rain started to slow and Nixie hoped it was enough to get the fires under control, because she couldn't dance again. Not with Graham lying dead in her arms and his blood staining the concrete of the roof.

"Ryan!" Peyton's shout drew their attention and they turned to look at her. Her hands were clenched into fists at her side. Willow and Julian stood just behind her. When they saw Graham's body, they pushed past her and rushed to Nixie's side.

The gun clattered to the ground.

"It's too late," Nixie said through her tears. "I'm sorry, I'm so sorry," she sobbed. She didn't know when the tears had started. Hard to tell through the rain, but she felt them now, coursing hotly down her cheeks.

"Shh, it's okay," Julian said, pulling her into his arms and away from Graham. Willow leaned down and closed his eyes, which made her sob only harder.

"If it wasn't for me, he'd still be alive."

"Stop that. He did what he had to do."

"But he shouldn't have been here."

"It was his job to look after you, Nixie. He was a guard."

That caught her attention. "No he isn't." *Wasn't.* "He's a forager. He told me—"

"I know that's what he told you." Julian helped her to her feet. "But he was a guard, same as me and Peyton. Same as Enrique."

She wanted to argue with him, but she just shook her head. She fell into Peyton's outstretched arms and buried her face against the wet fabric of her shirt. She was inexplicably exhausted, and she wanted to sleep for days. "I'm sorry. I didn't mean for Graham to get hurt."

"It's not your fault. Ryan pulled the trigger, not you. He's with Dad, now. Wherever they are."

Nixie pulled back. "I thought you didn't believe in things like that."

Her guard shrugged a shoulder, kissed the top of her head, and looked up. "No, but it sounded pretty, didn't it?"

CHAPTER THIRTY-SIX

It would take months of work to repair the damage to two of the apartments that had received the brunt of the fire damage. A few others suffered only minor smoke damage, thanks to their quick-thinking inhabitants. Peyton surveyed each one with Cooper, helping him make a list of the materials they would need.

Some of the Scavengers had stepped forward, offering to help as a way of apology, and with Nixie as their go-between, Old Joe agreed that they could have limited access to the settlement while they helped repair the damage. And once the work was completed, they'd discuss long-term arrangements.

Peyton sat on the windowsill of the tower, watching everyone work below her. In the wake of Graham's death, Old Joe had ordered her to take time off from her guard duties. She'd protested, but there was no arguing with the old man. So there she sat.

Ryan had been taken away. Again, another thing she wasn't allowed to be involved with. Old Joe worried she would kill him, and he was probably right. Scary to think about how much she'd thought of taking another's life in the last few days. A creak on the steps alerted her to another's presence, and she turned to find Nixie watching her, looking radiant in the dress Avery had given her, the same one she'd worn that night at Graham's for dinner. She smiled and held out an arm. Nixie quickly crossed the floor and leaned into her, stretching up for a kiss.

And I was ready to send her away. I must be crazy.

"Are you coming?" she asked, propping her chin on Peyton's shoulder as she turned to look back out the window. People were working in the abandoned building across the way, converting it to new apartments for the Scavengers who would be joining the Mill once the trial period was over. One of them spotted her and waved before ducking back inside.

"Yeah."

"Dr. Easton said Ranger is doing fine, and he can have visitors now. She said he's been complaining since he woke up. He hates being confined."

"This must be torture for him, then."

"I'm sure it is."

Peyton slid from her perch and slipped her fingers through Nixie's, tightening her grip. Nixie returned the squeeze and she smiled. She wasn't going to let Nixie out of her sight again.

The heavy door to the medical wing was shut, but that didn't stop the loud voices within. Peyton raised an eyebrow and looked down at Nixie who rolled her eyes. "Oh, boy."

"Hey!" Jasper called, jogging down the hall to catch up. "Is he allowed visitors yet?"

"We were just going to see him." Peyton opened the door and let the three of them in. Dr. Easton stood in one doorway, arguing loudly with the occupant.

She turned to them and threw up her hands. "I can't do anything with this one," she muttered. "He's all yours. Just keep him in bed. I had to tie a strap to his legs. The sedative should kick in eventually. You should get a few minutes. I need to check on Avery and baby Graham."

"This has to be against your doctor's code or something!" Ranger protested. Nixie stifled a laugh behind her hand and Peyton followed her into the room with Jasper at her heels. "Nix, help me get this off."

"I think you have to stay in bed. Doctor's orders."

"This is inhumane," he moaned, tugging at the strap across his legs. The buckle had been placed on the side of the bed closest to his injured arm so he wouldn't be able to reach it.

"I'm sure she'd take it off if you stayed where you were supposed to," Peyton said. She propped herself up on the counter as Nixie sat in the chair by the bed. The man sighed and dropped his head onto the pillow.

"How are you feeling?" Nixie asked.

"I've been better," he said softly. He looked at his bandaged arm and Peyton followed his gaze. Not only was it wrapped in cloth, but the arm had been bound against his body to keep it still. "Dr. Easton says I probably won't be able to use my arm again." His voice broke a little as he said it, and he cleared his throat. "Not much, at least. Won't be much of a help around here."

"You saved my life," Peyton said with conviction. "It doesn't matter what you can or can't do. You have a place here."

Jasper hadn't said a word, but he moved closer to the head of the bed. "You're lucky. If it had hit more to the left it would have pierced your heart."

"It should have," Ranger argued, tilting his head back to look at Jasper. "I would have deserved it after what I did to Peyton's father, but I guess this is the punishment I get for—"

His words were cut off as Jasper leaned down and pressed a kiss to his lips, silencing him. Nixie and Peyton looked to each other, stunned, and turned back as Jasper broke the kiss.

Ranger didn't say a word and Jasper grinned triumphantly. "It works! I've been wanting to try that out," Jasper crowed.

"You're an idiot." Peyton shook her head and reached out to take Nixie's hand.

"Should we leave the two of you alone?" Nixie teased.

Jasper had his fingers in Ranger's short hair, and he grinned widely. "Not that much would get accomplished. Dr. Easton would kill me."

Ranger's eyes drooped and he yawned. "That feels nice," he murmured before whatever sedative the doctor had given him kicked in.

"Magic fingers," Jasper whispered, holding up his free hand and wiggling the digits.

The outer door banged open and Dr. Easton yelled, "For the love of—Static! Will you please be careful? This is a medical ward, not some party house!"

"Sorry! So sorry!" Static practically ran into the room, ignoring everyone's attempts to slow him down and keep him quiet.

"Static, what the hell is your problem?" Peyton pushed off the counter and grabbed his shirt collar, ready to haul him out of the room, but he broke free of her grasp and held out the radio in his hands.

"I got it to work!" He pushed the medical equipment aside and set it down carefully. "I've been looking everywhere for you, and Willow said Jasper was headed here, so I figured you'd be here, too. I had to show you, before everyone else. Because you helped me. But I did it."

"Wha—?" Ranger tried to speak but Jasper hushed him while Peyton tried to get Static to lower his voice. It was no use.

"Listen!" he cried as he switched the radio on.

Nothing happened. Peyton sighed.

"Static—"

A faint, scratchy sound came out of the speakers, and Static turned the volume up.

Peyton could hear it clearly now. "It works."

"Told you it would."

"What does it mean?" she asked.

Static started to explain, but before he could get far, a voice interrupted them.

If you...hear...not alone.

Everyone stared at the radio, mouths open in shock.

"It's someone's talking," Peyton whispered. Static hushed her and she listened. He fiddled with one of the dials just a little, carefully nudging it with a steady hand.

The voice returned.

If you can hear us, you're not alone. This is Maverick from Farmington, Connecticut. CB radio channel two.

"Maverick," Jasper whispered, glancing at Static. "Can it be...?" Static stared at him, mouth open.

Peyton turned and they all looked at each other, silent as the voice droned on in the background, giving more information. Static recovered from his shock, found a discarded pencil, and scribbled furiously on the rough counter. Finally he turned, his eyes wide.

"It's true. There are others out there. Maverick's out there." He let the words settle over the room before adding, "We can reconnect."

Peyton glanced down at her hands enjoined with Nixie's and smiled. They'd come a long way since that day Nixie fell into the river, and the future stood before them with endless possibilities. Tugging her girl closer, Peyton wrapped an arm around her shoulders and kissed the top of her head. Nixie looked up, her cool blue eyes crinkled at the corners with delight. "Some of us already have."

About the Author

While growing up, Jennifer Lavoie wanted to be a writer or a teacher and briefly debated a career in marine biology. The only problem with that was her fear of deep water. Starting during a holiday season as temporary help, she worked in a bookstore for six years and made it all the way up to assistant manager before she left to take a job teaching. Jennifer has her bachelor's degree in secondary English education and found her first teaching job working with middle school students. Along with another teacher and a handful of students, Jennifer started the first Gay-Straight Alliance at the school. She has since moved to another school, but is still active in student clubs and enjoys pairing students with books that make them love to read. Jennifer lives in Connecticut with her cat, Scout.

Soliloquy Titles From Bold Strokes Books

The First Twenty by Jennifer Lavoie. Peyton is out for revenge after her father is murdered by Scavengers, but after meeting Nixie, she's torn between helping the girl she loves and the community that raised her. (978-1-62639-414-8)

Taking the Stand by Juliann Rich. There's a time for justice, then there's a time for taking the stand. And Jonathan Cooper knows exactly what time it is. (978-1-62639-408-7)

Fifty Yards and Holding by David-Matthew Barnes. The discovery of a secret relationship between Riley Brewer, the star of the high school baseball team, and Victor Alvarez, the leader of a violent street gang, escalates into a preventable tragedy. (978-1-62639-081-2)

Dark Rites by Jeremy Jordan King. When friends start experimenting with dark magic to gain power, Margarite must embrace her natural gifts to save them. (978-1-62639-245-8)

Driving Lessons by Annameekee Hesik. Dive into Abbey Brooks's sophomore year as she attempts to figure out the amazing, but sometimes complicated, life of a you-know-who girl at Gila High School. (978-1-62639-228-1)

Asher's Shot by Elizabeth Wheeler. Asher Price's candid photographs capture the truth, but when his success requires exposing an enemy, Asher discovers his only shot at happiness involves revealing secrets of his own. (978-1-62639-229-8)

The Melody of Light by M.L. Rice. After surviving abuse and loss, will Riley Gordon be able to navigate her first year of college and accept true love and family? (78-1-62639-219-9)

Maxine Wore Black by Nora Olsen. Jayla will do anything for Maxine, the girl of her dreams, but after becoming ensnared in Maxine's dark secrets, she'll have to choose between love and her own life. (978-1-62639-208-3)

Bottled Up Secret by Brian McNamara. When Brendan Madden befriends his gorgeous, athletic classmate, Mark, it doesn't take long for Brendan to fall head over heels for him—but will Mark reciprocate the feelings? (978-1-62639-209-0)

Searching for Grace by Juliann Rich. First it's a rumor. Then it's a fact. And then it's on. (978-1-62639-196-3)

Dark Tide by Greg Herren. A summer working as a lifeguard at a hotel on the Gulf Coast seems like a dream job…until Ricky Hackworth realizes the town is shielding some very dark—and deadly—secrets. (978-1-62639-197-0)

Everything Changes by Samantha Halc. Raven Walker's world is turned upside down the moment Morgan O'Shea walks into her life. (978-1-62639-303-5)

Tristant and Elijah by Jennifer Lavoie. After Elijah finds a scandalous letter belonging to Tristant's great-uncle, the boys set out to discover the secret Uncle Glenn kept hidden his entire life and end up discovering who they are in the process. (978-1-62639-075-1)

Caught in the Crossfire by Juliann Rich. Two boys at Bible camp; one forbidden love. (978-1-62639-070-6)

Frenemy of the People by Nora Olsen. Clarissa and Lexie have despised each other for as long as they can remember, but when they both find themselves helping an unlikely contender for homecoming queen, they are catapulted into an unexpected romance. (978-1-62639-063-8)

The Balance by Neal Wooten. Love and survival come together in the distant future as Piri and Niko face off against the worst factions of mankind's evolution. (978-1-62639-055-3)

The Unwanted by Jeffrey Ricker. Jamie Thomas is plunged into danger when he discovers his mother is an Amazon who needs his help to save the tribe from a vengeful god. (978-1-62639-048-5)

Because of Her by KE Payne. When Tabby Morton is forced to move to London, she's convinced her life will never be the same again. But the beautiful and intriguing Eden Palmer is about to show her that this time, change is most definitely for the better. (978-1-62639-049-2)

The Seventh Pleiade by Andrew J. Peters. When Atlantis is besieged by violent storms, tremors, and a barbarian army, it will be up to a young gay prince to find a way for the kingdom's survival. (978-1-60282-960-2)

Asher's Fault by Elizabeth Wheeler. Fourteen-year-old Asher Price sees the world in black and white, much like the photos he takes, but when his little brother drowns at the same moment Asher experiences his first same-sex kiss, he can no longer hide behind the lens of his camera and eventually discovers he isn't the only one with a secret. (978-1-60282-982-4)

Meeting Chance by Jennifer Lavoie. When man's best friend turns on Aaron Cassidy, the teen keeps his distance until fate puts Chance in his hands. (978-1-60282-952-7)

Lake Thirteen by Greg Herren. A visit to an old cemetery seems like fun to a group of five teenagers, who soon learn that sometimes it's best to leave old ghosts alone. (978-1-60282-894-0)

The Road to Her by KE Payne. Sparks fly when actress Holly Croft, star of UK soap *Portobello Road*, meets her new on-screen love interest, the enigmatic and sexy Elise Manford. (978-1-60282-887-2)

Swans & Klons by Nora Olsen. In a future world where there are no males, sixteen-year-old Rubric and her girlfriend Salmon Jo must fight to survive when everything they believed in turns out to be a lie. (978-1-60282-874-2)